Love's Gamble

The Brothers of Chi-Town, Book 8

WWW.CHERYLBARTON.NET

CHERYL BARTON

Dedication

This book is dedicated to the memory of my father, John A. Barton, Jr., who passed away on June 27, 2024 and to my brother, John A. Barton, III, who passed away on February 24, 2010. Both of you are forever in my hearts and my thoughts. You are missed every single day! Continue to rest sweetly until we meet again.

Dear Reader,

Here we are at the end of the road with, *The Brothers of Chi-Town*. Who would have thought that an idea I had for one book, the first in the series, *I Can't Let Go*, would turn into eight stories of unshakable, undeniable love. This series is why I love writing so much. Each story reflects the love of a man for a woman that leaves him with no doubt that she is the one for him. When the heart knows, it knows.

I hope you have enjoyed this amazing ride with me. If you haven't checked out all of the books in the series yet, make sure to get your read on. Each book stands alone, but I recommend reading them in order at

https://www.amazon.com/dp/B07Z4PRXBP?binding=kindle_edition&ref=dbs_dp_rwt_sb_pc_tkin.

I do believe you will find the entire series as one that you will love from the first page of book 1 to the very last page of book 8.

Thank you for being a big reason why I write. Readers are who make us writers shine and thrive. I thank you for my light.

As always, happy reading!

Cheryl Barton

About Love's Gamble

Tightly wound casino owner, Horace Grant didn't know what family meant until the day his best friend Torrence called him brother. Finding his footing in life in Las Vegas, he put the word 'sin' in "Sin City" with the wicked relationships with women that came with having money and power. Soon, that was no longer enough for him. Making a move to Chicago, his newfound friends showed him what was missing from his life; real, true love.

Angel Reagan has been a lost soul for most of her adult life. For years, she'd been running away from facing the bleak reality of life without her son who died and a family who made her feel nothing but shame. Having unconditional love was never something in her grasp until she met Horace, a man who cared for her like no other.

Horace and Angel are two broken souls who discover that life may not come at them straight with no chasers, but love can break through even the smallest crack in concrete.

Can Horace, who knows everything about gambling, trust his next gamble on his heart?

Prologue

"Prince? Where are you?"

"Horace, hang up the phone!"

The booming sound of his father deep voice that made the walls of their tiny house vibrate didn't deter him one bit. Horace was too focused on saving his only brother even if no one else would.

"No!" he yelled over his shoulder at his father where they both stood ten toes down in defiance against each other. Never had he stood up against his father in this manner, but this was about his brother who had struggled enough on his own. His father was such a hard ass that his idea of letting Prince learn his lesson in the streets wasn't the way he hoped he would go. Prince needed more. He needed someone in his corner.

When he heard his father's footsteps moving in his direction from the other side of the room, Horace ran from the living room, through the small dining room and into the kitchen. He moved to the opposite side of the square table and four chairs that had seen better days. When his hand gripped the back of one of the chairs, two of his fingers sank beyond the pleather, not leather top through one of many slits in the top of it.

Horace kept his eyes on the back door just in case his father came closer to him than what he wanted. He'd had his share of beatings from the man with a penchant for the right hand of the law against his kids. Today, he was fighting back with his disobedience. His breaths were ragged. His concentration was on the desperation he heard in his older brother's voice.

This wasn't Prince usual call for help. At eighteen, he was two years older than him. To his dismay, they were like night and day. Still, his father's treatment of Prince didn't sit well with him.

He and Prince never agreed on anything. Oftentimes, they fought like they were professional boxers in a ring. Even with their differences, no one understood Prince like he did; not his mother and *certainly* not his father.

Andrew Grant was a hard, cold man who didn't soften even when it came to his kids. He'd even heard him going after their mother, Cissy, a time or two. Horace hated that a part of his father. Truth be told, Horace started to see that coldness in himself that was making him too much like his father. Everything went to hell toward Prince when he developed an addiction to drugs. Their family had been through a lot in the past two years. Six months ago, his father told Prince to never come home again after their front door was kicked in by the police during their search for Prince on an outstanding warrant for drugs. His brother had missed another court date that had something to do with robbing a family at gunpoint in an effort to steal money and other items of value that he could trade in for drugs.

When he heard a low, guttural cough on the other end of the phone, Horace turned his attention back to Prince, but kept a watchful eye on his father.

"I'm tired, Horace. It's cold out here. I don't have any place to go. Can you sneak me in tonight? Just tonight. I promise I won't ask again. It's freezing cold out here at night."

Horace looked to his father who impatiently tapped the invisible watch on his wrist. That was his signal that he wanted the phone conversation to end. He didn't know what to do. He'd been going along with his father's plan of teaching Prince a lesson using tough love even though he didn't want to. If he helped his brother, that would mean suffering his father's wrath for him. If he sided with his father, he didn't know what would become of his brother. Horace was torn. At sixteen, these feelings were a lot for him to have to deal with. He had to make a choice. His father's stare and stance said that he had better make the right one or he could find himself out in the cold with his brother. He chose selfishly and prayed he wouldn't live to regret his choice.

Exhaling in defeat, he chose his battle.

"I can't, bro. I'll get in trouble. Don't you have friends you can stay with?" he asked Prince.

"Horace, this is your *last* warning to hang up that phone. Your brother made this bed and he can sleep on it."

"But, dad…"

He couldn't finish the conversation. With Prince speaking in the background and him trying to listen to at least calm him down, his father caught him unaware by reaching across the table and snatching the phone.

"Prince, stop calling here! Until you get the help you need, we can't do anything for you. I can't have your drugs in this house. You've brought us enough misery. Your mother is pregnant and at risk of losing the baby because of your antics. You're dragging this family down. Don't, *please* dad, me. I told you to get some help. Until you do, you are on your own. Do not call here again!"

Horace didn't know how to react. Who was this man?

Before he could stop his father, he watched him put the cell phone in his back pocket and walk away. He went after him.

"We're not going to help him?" he asked.

When his father's eyes landed on him with a gaze that was as cold as ice, Horace took a step back.

"I will tell you just like I told him; we have given him all the help we can. I've gone into debt paying for rehab stay, after rehab stay, only for him to leave after a few days. He's on his own. You had better mind your manners or you'll find yourself out there with him. This is my house and what I say goes. I don't want to hear of you speaking to him again while you're in this house."

Horace was on the brink of tears. He knew that he should have done more to help Prince long before now. He didn't like the sound of his voice or that nasty cough. What he heard was unlike any of their previous conversations.

"This is different. He sounded different. I think he's ready to get help. It's really cold outside, especially at night. He doesn't have anywhere else to go. He'll freeze out there. Please help him," Horace pleaded.

"I said *NO!* Lay off or go out there with him. Am I making myself clear? I don't want to hear his name in this house again unless he's been clean for at least a month. I'm going to pick your mother up from work. I suggest you get your school work done and not worry about your brother who, you forget, chose drugs over even you. He chose that over all of us. Why should we choose him first?" Andrew asked.

"Because he's your *son!*" Horace yelled.

He held his ground even when his father reached over and grabbed him up by his shirt, his feet actually leaving the

4

ground. The feel of the shirt being grabbed up around his neck was choking him. He gasped for breath. Seeing him struggle to breath didn't phase his father one bit.

"He's no son of mine. You should remember that the next time you disobey me or I won't know you either."

When his father let him go, he didn't just release his shirt. Horace was thrown to the ground where he fell back with his head slamming hard onto the floor. His vision blurred for a second as he tried to gather what had just happened. Before he could stand, his father had left the house, slamming the kitchen door behind him. He was happy he'd left out and not come for him for round two.

**

"No!"

A scream tearing through the house in the middle of the night woke Horace up out of shallow sleep. He'd hadn't had a deep sleep in a long time out of fear just being in this house. Hearing a second scream, he knew his mother's voice; even her screams. He'd heard them enough from her being on the other end of his father's fury. This was a different kind of scream. It was followed by a wailing that was from somewhere deep within; from her soul.

Jumping out of bed and hopping down from the top bunk where Prince used to sleep, Horace raced down the hall in his bare feet with the freezing cold wood floors not providing a barrier against the immediate chill that surfaced through his body, until he reached the top of the stairs. His heart was beating hard as if it would soon burst through his chest. He looked down the steps to see his mother crumpled to the floor with a police officer trying to calm her. His father stood tall, holding his uncaring posture, showing that nothing bothered him. Whatever was said had to be bad; *really* bad. Deep inside, he didn't want to know what happened. On the other hand, he knew he wouldn't be able to go back to bed without knowing. Not able to see his mother bent over and holding her growing belly where his baby sister was growing, he finally convinced his brain to tell his feet to move.

He took the steps slowly while already on the brink of tears just from his mother's howls. He wanted to comfort her, even if his father didn't see that she needed him more than he needed to continue being unmovable. Rubbing the knot on the back of his head, he remembered how it got there and decided to address his mother and not his father. He wondered if he had pushed his father to help his mother, if the man would strike out at him even in the presence of the police.

"Mom? What's wrong?" he asked, moving next to her, placing a protective hand on her back.

She didn't respond. She only cried harder and louder.

He looked from the officers to his father. Without even looking at him, his father directed his words over his shoulder.

"Your brother overdosed. He's gone."

Horace dropped to his knees after those few words stole his breath in an attempt to also steal the life right out of him. Prince was *gone*? He was *dead*? He knew his brother needed help. He knew it and instead of doing what was best for Prince by sneaking him in for a warm night, he did what his father said and ignored him and his pleas for help. How could he *ever* live with what happened now?

Holding on to his mother, Horace cried. Life wasn't supposed to be this hard. His mother should not have lost a son. His father should have cared more; and, so should he. This life was hard for him at home. No one knew it, but he was already planning his escape from this doom and gloom. Where he would go, he didn't know. It wasn't the time to be thinking of that. He needed to refocus on Prince. He let him down when he was alive. He wouldn't do it after his death. Grieving Prince the way that he should was first on his list. Following that, putting this life behind him would be next. He didn't have a plan, but if it meant being out in the world alone, he was willing to take that risk. He was willing to gamble with his life in order to find a better one.

1

"Horace?"

Feeling a hand patting his shoulder, Horace jumped to his feet in a state of confusion of where he was and what was happening around him. He staggered before remembering he was at the local precinct in Chicago. He started to remember as his mind shook off the dream and brought him back to reality. Now he got it. He was in a police station waiting with Joey and Marlow Kincaid, good friends of his. He'd driven them to the police station to check in on Marlow's sister, Angel who called her during a party at a friend's house. They were gathered with a large group of friends when panic and worry had Marlow in shambles after he handed her cell phone to her that had been ringing inside of the house. He also remembered the look on her face of sheer terror. He'd seen that before. That look reminded him of one of the last time's he'd seen his mother. It was the day they were notified that his brother had died. His mind had gone into protective gear. He couldn't help his mother all those years ago, but he could help Marlow, Joey and her sister.

"Are you okay?" Joey asked him. "I didn't mean to startle you awake," he added.

Horace gave Joey the thumbs up and kept the man's stare; his way of declaring he was okay after what must have seemed frightening when he was suddenly rocked awake. He must have looked like a madman. This wasn't the first time he'd relived the nightmare of losing his brother. There were times when he'd wake from that dream to wander into the bathroom of his Las Vegas apartment to see a wild looking man staring back at him; it was him. He was that wild looking man. That's probably how Joey saw him. Like many nights for the past seventeen years, his sleeping mind had taken him back to that night so long ago that still plagued him. Why he still couldn't shake that horrible time in his life, he didn't know. What he didn't know was that this moment wasn't about him. It was about Angel.

"Oh, um, yeah, I'm good. I must have dozed off without realizing it. How are things?" he asked, hoping to change the subject.

When Marlow walked up and put a protective arm around him, Horace gave her a reassuring smile. She had enough on her plate and didn't need to care for him too.

"Are you sure? You were saying the word, no, over and over and tossing a little," Marlow said.

He patted her hand to show he had already forgotten about the dream.

"I promise, I'm good. I've had a lot of long days and nights lately. How's your sister?" he asked.

Changing the subject was the best way for him to avoid having to address the tragedy that was his own life's story. Joey knew some of it, but he didn't think Marlow knew any of it. He'd shared his history with a group of his guy friends, but that was about it.

"She's okay. She looks pretty rough," Marlow said.

The sorrow in her voice worried him. He was used to seeing her laughing and smiling. The look on her husband's face told him that he wasn't the only one who was worried about her.

"We were able to get in to see her thanks to a friend who is a cop in this precinct who does some moonlighting work in security for Carlos and I," Joey said.

"She looks tired. She's being charged with abandonment of her daughter, Marleigh. The attorney your friend, Manny, sent is good. I think you said she's Manny's sister. Her name is Kris Mahomes. My sister, Angel, is also being charged with solicitation of a police officer. She says it's not true. This is a cop she says that has been trying to get in her pants for a while. She returned to Chicago almost a year ago before she had Marleigh. My niece is nine months old," Marlow explained.

"I don't know about you, but I believe Angel. She says it was a setup," Joey said. "I know we should believe all cops are trustworthy, but there are some snakes in the bunch. This cop, Charlie, seems to be that snake.

"I know my sister and she may be a lot of things, but a liar isn't one, so yeah, I believe her. If she says this cop set her up, that's exactly what happened," Marlow said.

Horace moved them to a corner so that they could keep an eye on anyone who may be trying to hear their conversation. After all, they were in a precinct full of cops.

"Is the cop out of this house?" Horace questioned.

"No. I asked that same question because I was concerned about her safety. He isn't. Apparently, when she wouldn't put out, he drove her past the city limits and told her to get out of the car. She threatened to turn him in and he told her if she did, she would never see her daughter again. By the time she made her way back to the house where she was staying with some older woman, the police were there and the woman said she'd had the baby for days. She claimed Angel hadn't been there in almost a week which is why she called the cops to come and see about the baby. Angel swears she only left Marleigh for a few hours, though it took her more hours to get back to the house. She believes the cop got to the woman and convinced her to lie to keep Angel quiet. There is a lot to this. Kris, is wielding her way through it all."

"Where's your niece?" Horace asked.

"The Department of Family and Children's Services or DFCS has her. That acronym is less of a mouthful to say. We were told that after Marleigh is officially checked over at a local hospital, she'll be placed in emergency foster care until everything is worked out. They won't tell us which hospital she was taken to."

Marlow paused. Horace knew that look. She was holding back tear.

"I'm sure this will all get sorted out and your sister will be out. I know you're worried about your niece."

Horace offered reassurance but wasn't sure it was working. There was a time in his youth that he had been told everything would work out and it didn't. He wanted to hope for a different outcome for Marlow and her sister.

"I want her, Joey. Please help me get my niece out of the system. That's no place for her. I failed Angel once with Angelo. He died in that swimming pool and didn't get to live a life beyond a toddler. I can't do that with Marleigh. I can't let anything happen to her in the hands of strangers. What if it does and we're not there?" Marlow cried.

Horace took one of her hands in his as she cried in Joey's arms. He watched Joey lean her back in order to speak directly into her eyes.

"Baby, listen to me. I don't care what it takes. We aren't going to let Marleigh stay in foster care. Don't forget that Kris said she would do everything in her power to get things expedited through family court. Angel isn't getting out tonight because of the additional assault charge. When she got back to the house and saw her baby being taken away, she tussled with a cop who says Angel assaulted her. It's all confusing. We'll go pick up Maia and go home to get some rest," Joey explained.

"No, I can't just leave her here," Marlow pleaded.

"We can't help her tonight. We did what we could and that is, thanks to Horace and his connections, she has a lawyer who can handle the cases against Angel along with the family court case. Let's trust that she knows what she's doing. Besides, this place has a putrid smell and the walls could use a coat of paint," Joey said, trying to lighten the mood by smiling at her and wiping away her tears.

The tender moment between them reminded Horace that when he ventured home at the end of the day, he didn't have a woman to comfort like this. Before meeting his Chicago friends and their wives, he didn't know how much he wanted that in his life now.

"You're right. I need to get out of here and go hug my baby. This makes me miss her even more since we've been here. Can you believe that my sister and I will have kids that will grow up together? Girls, even?" Marlow asked.

"I love it and I love you," Joey noted.

"I need to call my brother. He can tell my mother about all of this. I don't think I can deal with Delores tonight. We haven't told her that Angel has been calling us for months on end. I can only imagine how focused she will be on us not telling her that as opposed to being concerned about Angel and the baby," Marlow explained.

"Good idea. Let your brother deal with her. I don't want you stressed out. Maia will feel that in her little body when she's close to you. No stress, baby."

"Hey people!" Torrence said walking up to them.

After he greeted everyone, Horace caught his best friend's eyes checking to see if he was okay. Both of them knew why.

"Hey!" Horace replied, trying to put a cover over the feelings he could never hide from Torrence. They had been friends since he was sixteen or seventeen years old. If anyone knew him, Torrence did.

"You good?" Torrence asked him.

"Yeah, I'm good," Horace lied.

He saw the moment Torrence didn't believe him but was thankful his friend let it go for now.

"How's your sister?" Torrence asked Marlow.

"She's hanging in there. You're here? Where's Reese?" Marlow questioned.

"I got her and the baby settled in at home. She's good. She's worried about you. I promised her I would check-in."

"Mrs. Kincaid?"

They all turned in the direction of a female officer who showed up in the hallway.

"Yes?" Marlow anxiously responded.

"There are a few more questions for you. Can you follow me?"

"Yes. Joey?"

Marlow looked to him for support.

"He can come as well," the officer offered and turned in the direction she had come in.

"We'll be back. I know you're tired, Horace. We can get a rideshare home," Joey said.

"Nonsense. I'll be here when you're ready."

"So will I," Torrence added.

"Cool. I'll update you when we get back," Joey said rushing off to catch up with Marlow and the officer.

Horace looked to Torrence who looked back at him without even blinking.

"I know why you offered to jump in and help. You've been trying to rescue the needy for a lot of years. I can look at you and tell that this incident has taken you back in time. You know Angel's history of drug use. You also remember your brother's drug history. You look wiped out. Maybe you should leave and get some rest. I can wait for them," Torrence offered.

"No, I promise you, I'm alright. I fell asleep while I was waiting."

"Another nightmare?"

Horace nodded and sat down on the dark brown wooden bench with his elbows on both knees, his head hung low.

"I've been getting them more frequent lately."

"You know you couldn't save him, right? This has plagued you for a lot of years. I know I can say you should let it go but that wasn't my experience. Don't let this consume you, is all I'm saying. You have the biggest heart of anyone I've ever met. I don't want you to get overwhelmed."

"I've heard Marlow talk about what happened to her sister. When I heard about this, I guess Angel's story triggered old wounds for me. She's Marlow's sister who she tried to help several times to no avail. I tried that with Prince or at least I thought I was trying. I jumped into action."

Horace jumped up and paced from left to right, rubbing his hand down his beard, huffing out loud to relieve his unease.

"What gives? We've always been able to talk. We've been like brothers ever since you moved in with my family when you were seventeen years old. For a month, we shared the same room until my parents turned the guest bedroom into a room for you after my mother declared, she would fight to hell and back before she let you go back to your nightmarish life. We talk about everything in our lives. You seem unusually wound up. The nightmare of that night? Happened tonight?"

"I fell sleep right here on this bench. The dream was so real as if I was actually back there that night. My family was so dysfunctional."

"Yet, you turned out okay."

"Torrence, that's because of you and your family. You took me in and gave me the kind of family I wished I'd had; I wished my brother would have had a chance to have. I don't know. It's like being here in Chicago brings it all back."

"Chicago? Why?"

Horace hunched his shoulders and then released them, sighing knowing he needed to speak his truth.

"Being here, life is calmer than in Las Vegas. I feel drawn to go back so that the big lights, all night action and just loudness that is Vegas can distract me from thinking about life. Here and around all these powerful guys and their families, growing families, I might add, reminds me of what my life doesn't have. I still live a rogue life, though I now do it with a lot of money. I guess money really can't buy everything. Helping people brings me peace. Before meeting your friends and how they've included me as family, reminds me that I grew up never feeling wanted or needed. With this crowd, it's like they are all family. It feels good. I called your mom the other day. I just needed to hear her voice even though my mother is still alive and living in North Carolina now. All these great families remind me of what I missed out on."

"But you have a chance to have all that you want and need in life. You're thirty-three, co-owner of three casinos as well as other business ventures. How many of your good friends back in New York, North Carolina or even in Las Vegas can stay that they made their first million before they were thirty? Not many, but you sure can. You have women tossing themselves at you around the clock. I've never seen you short of having a bevy of beautiful woman around and in your bed. If you want more that bed buddies, you have to go for it. We are all your family. My mom told me she talked to you. She also said she was worried and that you should go home for a visit."

Horace smiled and laughed lightly. Torrence's mother always thought the answer to cure all ills was to come home to a week of her southern cooking and loving arms. She was right. He could use that. Maybe one day, he'll get up the nerve to visit his own mother. Going back to them didn't bring him comfort, though he missed his two younger sisters. He still wasn't ready.

"I may do that. I haven't visited your mom and dad since Christmas."

"Do that. Reese and I are thinking of going home for a visit to take the baby. Come go with us. It'll be good."

"I'll think about it. I need to make a stop in Vegas to check in on things."

Torrence shook his head at him, showing him all of his teeth in the most facetious grin he'd ever seen.

"You mean you're going back to see Ace, right?" Torrence assumed.

Horace hated to say that the woman was on his mind. Asia Wingate, better known as Ace, was as unforgettable as she was beautiful. Still, she was the party girl type, not the type you took home to introduce to the family. She could be though, considering the family she came from. The Wingate family is well known in Nevada. If he had been ready for more, it could have been with her. Something inside of him told him, she wasn't the one. Maybe no one was.

"She's been blowing up my phone about when I'm returning to Vegas. It's all fun, though. I have no doubt she's not letting her bed get cold. Ace isn't the type of woman to have one man in her life."

"That's why the two of you work because you aren't that type either. You and one woman? I can't imagine it," Torrence joked.

"Oh? There was a time when it seemed impossible for you too, but look at you now. You've got Reese, you're married and a father. You are committed to one woman, unless there is something you'd like to share?" Horace kidded.

"Oh, hell no. Absolutely not. Reese is it for me. She is more than enough woman for me and all of my needs. I love her with everything in me. I almost lost her by being mister swagger and then bringing all of my baggage into her life. When she forgave me, I promised that I was all about her and only her. I've never had a reason to think or do otherwise. I can't wait for the day when that happens for you. It will. Trust me."

"From your lips...well, you know the rest."

"You heard me say it first. The woman of your dreams will be that peace you're seeking. You won't have to gamble on whether love is out there for you. You'll know it. You still have a lot from your past you need to deal with."

Before they could continue their conversation, Joey and Marlow returned.

"Well?" Torrence asked them.

"We'll come back in the morning. Kris is going to push for Marleigh to be released to us through family court. She's also working out a game plan to get Angel released on bail tomorrow until her court date. If she can do that in the morning, she believes that she can get us before a judge in family court within the next few days. Until then, she's going to see if there is a way to get us in to see Marleigh."

"That's great news. I hope that helps!" Horace exclaimed. "That's something, huh?"

"It is great news. Kris said, if we can't get in to see her, she would. She could put in a legal request to check on the health and safety of Marleigh. That gave me comfort. Knowing Angel will be out tomorrow will help me get some sleep tonight. Let's all get out of here and get some rest. We'll be back in the morning to find out what's next. Angel felt better by the end of the conversation knowing that Marleigh could potentially be with us. All thanks to my wonderful husband who didn't even hesitate over the idea of bringing the baby home with us if and when we can."

Horace watched Joey kiss Marlow slow and reassuring like.

"I would move this earth out of orbit just for you," Joey declared for them all to hear.

When they all turned to head toward the entrance of the police station, Horace lagged behind, walking slower than them. Torrence was right. These people were more than friends, they were all family. The interaction he sees every day between his friends and their wives is admirable. It's not fake.

It's not forced. It's as real as real could ever be. Torrence's parents were the first he saw share real love between man and woman; husband and wife. Knowing that, he was no longer planning on being on the outside of life and watching it happen around him. Family helped family. He was ready for the task of doing just that, even for a woman he had never met. He felt drawn to her. Through his friends, he would help her in any way possible. He stood on the sidelines and watched life happen to Prince. If Marlow and Joey needed him to help with her sister, he's shifting from the sidelines and into action.

2

Angel didn't sleep well the night before. The notion that she was behind bars and could actually see bars was a sleep deterrent.

She was in her second day of wearing the same clothes, a short black skirt, black top under a fake leather jacket and black heels that were not as high as she liked to wear. She no longer owned shoes that were high and stylish. Her attire, these days, was more of what she could afford as opposed to what she desired to have. Attire aside, because she didn't care about it, she had other worries that caused her to have a morning migraine because she was full of worry. Her life was once again on a downward spiral. She hated that. Most of all, she missed her baby. To her, Marleigh was snatched away for no reason other than she trusted a woman, who up until yesterday, had been nothing but nice to her and Marleigh.

Laying back on the bunk in her cell, she was preparing to spend even more hours contemplating how life continued to kick her in the ass. Even when she'd finally gotten herself on a better path, especially after having Marleigh, she still couldn't get ahead. There was always someone or something that kept her down. It felt like being in a hole and every time she found a way to crawl out, someone's foot would smash her back down in to the hole, covering up her only way out with a mound of heavy dirt. Life was too much for her.

At twenty-five, she still couldn't get things together. While others lived happy, successful lives, she was stuck on stupid after trusting yet another man. He was just a line of many that she'd encountered in life so far.

First there was Santiago Vega who was never around for her despite his promise that he would be. She'd met him at a young age. She saw herself in the role of a military wife and thought she'd hit the jackpot. Her inability to kick her drug habit, especially after giving birth to their son Angelo, ruined everything good she thought that life could be.

There had been quite a few men after him who only used her for her body, something that took her a long time to figure out. That's why when she had been consistently approached by the same crooked police officer again and again after her return to Chicago, she fought hard to say no and stick to it. She'd already had a one-night-stand with a guy she'd met at a party in Miami and ended up pregnant, to her surprise. She never saw him again and had no clue of how to reach him. Still, she was pregnant and her baby was all that mattered. She knew she had to do that drug-free. She wanted something better for Marleigh.

Her plan was to move back to Chicago and reach out to her family for help and support. Pride kept her from doing that. She wanted to make something of herself before walking back into their lives. Instead, she ended up in a rut yet again. The only person she could think of to call was her sister when things finally crashed and burned. Thank goodness Marlow had never changed her cell phone after all the years. Ghosting her family again and again, Angel was ecstatic that Marlow was forgiving. She didn't deserve a great sister like her. She'd done wrong by Marlow. She was ready to make a change.

Dealing with Charlie, someone she thought she could trust had woken her up.

Angel grew up thinking that the police were the good guys. She'd met Charlie one day while out walking with Marleigh. Since that first meeting, he had been riding her hard for a date. She really thought he was different. He would show up at places where she hadn't told anyone she'd be; not even the woman who'd taken her and Marleigh in for a few dollars a month.

To help take care of Marleigh, she'd applied for public assistance which was easy to get since she was unemployed and pregnant. After having the baby, she'd found a night time job working at a local Chicago strip club as a waitress and sometimes dancer. Not as a stripper because she refused to take off her clothes. The owner was okay with that because he said her beauty would be a draw for the men at the club. She didn't need to take her clothes off to help him make money. He just wanted her to be seen. She was often told that she had the perfect body and looks that men wouldn't be able to resist. A few times, she looked out and saw Charlie in the club, hiding under a hat and high-collar jacket, making himself barely noticeable. Then the stalking started.

After weeks of pressing her for a date; what she thought was a real date, last night had happened. In the car, his true intentions became clear. That's when she'd had enough. She didn't know who to trust. His beady eyes should have been her warning. The night before, he'd pushed the limit with her. His plan was some hotel far from Chicago. She defied what he wanted from her and screamed *NO* more times than she could count. That angered him. She then became afraid that he would harm her. Just when she was thinking of a plan to jump out of the car while it was moving, he stopped and made her get out, telling her that she'd better keep her mouth shut. That all happened after she told him that she believed he was married. She hadn't picked up on it before but the way he was acting was a sure sign. In the car, she looked at his left hand and could clearly see that he usually wore a wedding ring. Last night, he must have taken it off and hid it from her like he had been doing all along. When her light bulb went off, it really went off. Everything about him and the situation became clear. She was willing to blow up his life to get him to leave her alone. That had angered him and now, she was in jail.

"Your lawyer is here," the female guard from the night before walked up and declared.

Angel leaped up and raced toward the metal bars of her cell. It had been a long night after her sister and brother-in-law left. Her lawyer had stayed a little longer with a promise that they would be back in the morning.

Once the cell door was opened, she pushed her way through it and turned down the hall in the direction that the officer pointed out to her. At the end of the hall, she entered the room that she'd been in the night before. Not only was her lawyer here, but so was Marlow and her brother Steven. The moment he saw her, he began to cry and pulled her into a big hug. She cried along with him. It had been too long. Once Marlow joined in on the hug, time stood still as they held on to each other.

"How are you?" Steven asked.

Angel pulled away and wiped her face with the back of her hand. She couldn't describe the feeling of being with Marlow and Steven again. So much had happened over the past few years. Being back home, even with her troubles, was best.

"Smelly, I bet. I haven't showered and that cell is nasty," she said, trying to joke. "Other than that, I'm doing okay. It's good to see you."

Steven was so elated to see her that he pulled her back into another tight hug and held on.

"I'm sorry," he whispered.

He was apologizing. She cried again, not for her, but for the guilt she knew he was also carrying around each day.

"Steven, don't. It's not your fault. It was all me," she said.

"No, it was all me. I introduced you to substances at a young age. I gave you beer. I gave you weed. You couldn't shake it because of what I did. I'm so sorry, sis. I miss you. I love you. I'm so, so sorry for how things have turned out," he lamented.

Angel took both of his hands into hers and held on.

"No more talk of that. It's all in the past. I promise you that nothing that has happened recently has anything to do with that. I've been clean since right before I got pregnant with Marleigh. Angelo dying had me out of control and things got worse. Marleigh was my saving grace. I just couldn't face life here at home after Angelo's death. I still had struggles, but it wasn't around substance abuse. They tested me last night. I know it will come back clean. Let yourself off the hook after all of this time. I hope you haven't been beating yourself up all these years," Angel said.

"He has. So have I. We are quite the family, huh?" Marlow asked.

Angel joined hands with both of them.

"I came back here because I was working on myself. I wanted to be in my best shape before I reached out. Then this happened. I trusted the wrong people. Again, that is on me. I had my daughter and I woke up. I stopped running. I stopped doing a lot of things. I didn't abandon her. It had only been a few hours, not days. I was away longer when I worked. I had just stopped that two days ago because I was tired of the grimy men; and some women. I don't know why Ms. Mable is lying. Charlie had to get to her to keep me from spilling that he was married and trying to get between my legs. I was terrified. I was willing to jump out of that car to get back to my daughter. He's lying," Angel confessed.

"That's why I'm here. I'm going to get all of this cleared up. Your initial hearing for bail is in a few hours. I've told your family what to expect after you told me last night that I can talk to your sister about everything," Kris said.

"Yes, thanks for doing that. I don't want them in the dark about anything anymore. If I'm going to be in trouble, I don't want my daughter caught up in this."

"I've got this covered," Kris confirmed.

"Marlow, what about my daughter? If I don't get out of here, will you take Marleigh? Please don't leave her in the system. She needs to be with family, especially if it's not me," Angel pleaded.

"I got her, just like I've got you," Marlow explained. "Joey and I already talked about that. I don't want you to worry."

"Let's all have a seat and let me explain what I'm working on," Kris said.

"I hope it's something that will get me out of here," Angel exclaimed.

"I'm hoping so. The issue is that you can't go back to where you were. That's the woman who said you abandoned your daughter with her," Kris said.

"She can come home with me and my husband. We have plenty of space and it's a stable home. Plus, if we get Marleigh, they will be together," Marlow said. "We plan to make room for Angel to stay at our house for as long as she needs to."

"That may be an option but it depends on whether or not family court will agree to Angel being in the home with her daughter until this is all resolved."

"Well, if that's not an option, my sister can come stay with me. I live in an apartment, but it has two bedrooms and she is more than welcome to use the other one. I have plenty of space. We are willing to do anything to get my sister out and someplace safe," Steven jumped in and spoke up.

Angel smiled when he reached and held onto her hand, this time, not letting it go.

"I'll note that, as well," Kris acknowledged. "I'm sure I can get you out on bail, though I don't know how much that will be. Do you all have funds for that?"

Angel shook her head from side-to-side and then turned to Marlow, who nodded and smiled.

"I have it. My husband has given me a blank check to pay whatever it will take to get Angel out on bail. We will take full responsibility for her and will make sure she follows any instructions issued by the court. What about Marleigh? If we can't get her right now, can I see her to make sure she's alright? I know Angel can't but someone in my family should be able to get eyes on her. What would we need to do?" Marlow asked.

"I've thought about options. Here is what I think we should do. I'm going to get Angel out on bail. I think we're in a good position to do that. I've reached out to child and family services about a court date and they were able to get us in tomorrow morning for an emergency hearing."

"Really? How did that happen so fast? I'm surprised," Marlow said.

"Very true. It is fast. I actually tossed out who your husband is, Marlow, and that if the baby could be placed with you and him, we should get a court date and get that settled. The system would rather have her with family than add another child to a temporary situation that's not family. I explained that Marleigh has family and shouldn't be placed in foster care. They were able to get a judge to squeeze us in. I'm hoping we can get your daughter tomorrow. Truth is, I doubt if the judge will hand her back over to Angel until the legal issues she's facing are resolved. I do believe they will release her to you and your husband with temporary custody. Maybe not tomorrow because there is a process. I don't think they will have an issue with Angel staying with you but custody will go to you and your husband. That will mean, you have to oversee Angel and Marleigh. There will be strict stipulations about Marleigh being in Angel's care alone. It will seem odd considering she's your daughter, but do what the court says and think about your daughter before you think about yourself and your needs. Understand?" Kris asked.

Angel wanted to hop up and do a dance. This was all great news as far as she was concerned. She would do anything to get her daughter out of the system while also getting to see her each day even if her sister and brother-in-law get custody. She was still wrapping her head around the fact that her brother-in-law was Joey Kincaid, also known as Joey Dreads, who was recently named the sexiest man alive, according to her chat with her sister the night before. She knew that he was not only good looking but also a good man.

"I will do any and everything I'm told. What happened with the drug tests? I already know, but I want you to tell my sister and brother," Angel professed.

"You are correct when you said the test would come back clean. I was sent that information just this morning. One strike against the woman who confirmed Officer Charles Miles' story. She told the police that she'd seen you doing hard drugs recently. That's clearly a lie. It will be interesting what she will say when she's called to testify, eventually, and I get to cross examine her. That will work in your favor. Still, the courts here in Chicago are tough. You will have to prove your worthiness when it comes to be trusted. I'm sure the story will come out in regards to what happened to your son and your drug use back then. We'll tackle that. The best thing you have going for you is your big group of friends by way of your sister and of course, your brother and sister being here for you. I received a call from our mayor this morning. The mayor of Chicago called me and asked what he could do." Kris turned to Marlow and smiled along with giving her a high-five. "How in the world do you know him?" she asked of Marlow.

Angel's eyes turned to Marlow who was grinning from ear to hear.

"Let me tell you about the group of friends I married into. Tucker Glass is a good friend of Joey, his brother, Carlos and their other brothers by relationship, but not by blood. I call them the *Brothers of Chi-Town*. One day, I'll run the entire list down to you. You didn't get to meet Torrence, who was here last night. His wife Reese is the big sister of the mayor's wife, Nichelle. Either Reese or Torrence must have told him about all of this," Marlow explained.

Angel gasped happily.

"Well damn. Do you know Barack and Michelle Obama too? I need to meet all of these friends. I see you sis! You know some people," Angel cheered.

"Yes, I do. Torrence is also business partners with Horace who drove us here like a bat out of hell last night after you called me. I'm telling you these guys and their wives are the greatest bunch of people I've ever met. Well, they're all married except for Horace. He was the first to leap into action to get us here. He stayed pretty much all night until we left together," Marlow said.

"Well, with all of these people in your corner, that gives us an upper hand that I plan to use. Just to recap, the plan is to get Angel out on bail with a promise that she'll be staying with Marlow and her husband. Any testing, visits or counseling the court mandates, you will follow. You will also not miss any scheduled court dates. That would put the money your family is putting up for you at risk of being seized. I believe you're innocent. Trust me to fight this battle for you to get you back to your life with your daughter. That's the priority. Are we on the same page with that?" Kris asked.

Angel heard the warning and was for anything that would get her back to her baby.

"Yes, I'm onboard. I appreciate your help. Please thank whoever recommended you. You are ready for battle!" Angel boldly declared.

"That was Horace," Marlow interrupted.

"What?" Angel asked.

"She's right. Horace and my brother Manny back from their college days. I believe they're in the same fraternity. Manny called me and told me to get to the police station immediately. He told me the little bit that Horace told him and that was all I needed. My brother and I are all we have, so we're close. When he calls and needs me for anything, I'm there," Kris explained.

Angel looked to Steven and Marlow and sorrow took over. Her own brother and sister have tried to reach out to her to lend their support for a long time and she just didn't answer them. She was anxious to get back to them being an awesome trio.

"I'm sorry guys. I know I've caused you a lot of stress. Thank you for being on the other end of the phone when I was finally able to reach out. I'm sorry it's for another issue," Angel admitted.

"It's okay. After hearing everything last night and today, I'm with Kris in that I believe you. We'll get this all sorted out so that we can be a family again. Besides, we have daughters who are about to be best friends."

"That's for sure. Imagine me being uncle and one of Maia's godfathers," Steven said, pumping his chest like King Kong.

"Marleigh could use you as her godfather too as long as Marlow doesn't mind sharing," Angel said.

"Sounds perfect to me, sis," Marlow declared.

"Me too," Steven added.

"Great. Let's go over a few more things and then you'll be brought before a judge for a bail hearing within the hour. Are you ready?" Kris asked.

With Marlow's hand in one of hers and Steven's hand in her other, she was ready for anything.

"Absolutely," Angel decreed. "Do I have to go back to that cell?"

"No. We can talk for the next hour to prevent that. When you're called, we'll go from here. I can only imagine what that's like," Kris said.

"After today, I hope I never have to find out again."

Angel meant that with everything in her.

3

While chatter from the architecture, design and construction leads behind him was going on, Horace checked out every detail of the main floor of the casino before any machines or other items were added. The three casino cages on the first of the three casino levels were definitely secure and private. He liked the additional security booths with one-way glass that were located on both sides of each cage. As he walked, he kept his eye on the floor plan as he tried picturing the large space with all of the gaming tables and machines occupied with guests twenty-four hours a day, seven days a week.

Though this isn't the first casino that he and Torrence have partnered on, this is the one that he holds closest to his heart because the final design was left up to him to work out with the architects. In a few more days, the space would be filled and he'd be taking another look at everything from the machines, poker tables, roulette wheels and to the seating and restrooms. There was still a lot that needed to be done and approved before the grand opening in a few months. Currently, his team was planning the grand event to be held the night before the casino opening that would be family oriented. The invite list consisted of local and national politicians, celebrities and most important to him, family and friends. The minute the word, family, went through his mind, he dismissed it. He had no family to invite.

"What do you think, boss?"

Cliff, one of the new casino managers he brought with him from the Las Vegas casino, caught up with him while the others talked while they continued to follow him.

"I think everything looks great. This is the first time we decided to go with a black and gold color scheme, which I really like," Horace said.

"I agree. When we met in Las Vegas the night you asked if I was interested in moving to Chicago to be one of the four managers of the new casino, I was a little skeptical about the choice of colors. As usual, you were right. The place looks rich, as it should."

"Yeah, I must say it was a great choice. Everything looks good. I'm glad we changed the carpet. I was hoping the internal signs would be up by now. I'm not sure what's taking that so long," Horace said.

He turned his head and when the men behind him nodded, he knew they'd heard him.

"We're working on that, Horace," Glenn Adams, the man from the lighting crew said. "My team will have those up for you tomorrow morning. What did you think of the outside signage? Pretty good, huh? It will look even better the night we light them all up. You'll be able to see the casino name from another planet!" Glenn added.

Everyone nodded and laughed. Horace was glad about that. His plan was falling in place. The bright, gold lettering will be seen from miles away.

"Man, do you ever take a break from this place? I knew I would find you here."

Horace dropped his head and laughed. He forgot that he and Joey were meeting today until he walked up with his cocky bowlegged strut.

"And I thought you'd be home under your wife since you'll be out of town soon," Horace acknowledged as they greeted each other.

After Joey shook the hand of each man, Horace attempted to introduce him to the few men in the group who he wasn't sure had ever met Joey before.

"Guys, this here is the man of the hour!" Horace gloated.

"Don't even go there, Horace," Glenn shouted. "There isn't a man in this room who doesn't know who Joey Dreads is!" he noted.

"Thanks for that," Joey said. "I appreciate it. Things are looking pretty good around here. You're still ahead of schedule?" he asked Horace.

"Yes, by a few weeks. We're still about three months out. I'm going to keep the grand opening date even if we are ahead of schedule with everything. That will give us room for anything that comes up that needs addressing. We're not in a rush but I don't want any lag time either. I want everyone to keep on schedule, even if it's days ahead. We'll have the final inspection in two months. The office space is complete. The hotel space above the casino floors is ready to be occupied on opening night. Listen, let's go into my office and talk," Horace offered. "You guys can continue to walkthrough and note anything that needs an adjustment. Cliff, stay with them. You and I can connect later on before I leave."

"You mean, if you leave?" Cliff joked. "I'm convinced you already live here."

"Nah, I still have my suite at the original hotel. I haven't decided on moving or not moving yet. I'm sure I'll have some kind of digs here just for those nights when I don't feel like going home. Anyway, hit my cell if you need anything pronto. Otherwise, let's go over anything you find when we chat."

"Sounds good boss."

Horace and Joey headed for the private elevators that went up four floors to the executive offices. That space had been completed three weeks ago.

"Will I get a chance to see the entertainment hall where the wrestling matches will be before I leave?" Joey asked.

"Definitely. We're good to go there. The final inspection is in two weeks. It's in great shape for you to see. You know, I appreciate you agreeing to be our first big event after the opening. I know you did that for the other casino and you were such a draw that we had to turn people away because we were at capacity in the casino, the hotel and in the hall. I will say, we are already sold out on tickets and hotel rooms for that night. Torrence is already working on accommodating people at the other casino and providing transportation to make it easier for people to get around."

Horace guided them to his office once the elevator arrived on the executive level. There were a few people milling about answering phones and continually working on the planned opening night festivities. He was looking forward to a night of celebrating success, not just when it came to the casino, but in life in general. The world has been a mad, mad place to be lately. He was happy to be a part of providing a break from bleakness to focus on fun and enjoyment.

"Horace, you and Torrence have outdone yourselves with this place. I can't wait to get into that new ring. My creative team is working on the game plan for that night. I'll tell you because I know you can keep a secret – we're bringing Carlos out that night. We're dusting off his persona for a major show for the fans who have been asking for him at every match. It's going to be epic!" Joey proclaimed.

Horace turned around sharply in excitement the minute they reached his office.

"Seriously? You're kidding, right? Do you know how big that's going to be to have the brothers together again? I never thought you'd ever be able to get your brother back in the wrestling ring."

Horace pointed to the black and gold leather seating area where they could sit and chat. As he sat, Horace ran his hand over the new black leather side chair with gold accents. Joey sat across from him in the three-seat sofa in black with the same accents. When he was thinking of the color scheme for the casino, he wanted to be sure his office was an exact match.

"Me either, but he agreed. I'm going to chalk it up to the many great friendships my brother and I have developed with the group of brothers here in Chicago. Torrence is one of the anchors of the friendship. He, along with the others, have welcomed my brother and I into the fold with open arms. Did you know that Carlos and I tried to kill Alyssa's husband, Dexter, when we first met him? Not actually kill him but we took our frustration out on him over his relationship with Alyssa. It was a crazy time."

Horace chuckled.

"I heard a little something about that. I understand it happened in Las Vegas. I would have loved to have seen that brawl."

"Yeah, that was something. When our sister showed up pregnant by a man she was no longer with, we thought that he'd knocked Alyssa up and then abandoned her. Considering the training Carlos and I have had, Dex held his own pretty good when he showed up out of nowhere. Once it was all worked out and Dex actually worked his ass off to get back into Alyssa's good graces and to claim his child, we became best buddies. I never thought that I would say it but, he turned out to be the perfect guy, provider, husband and father that any woman could ask for. Well, there is me of course, when it comes to loving my wife and daughter" he joked.

"I think I've gotten my head wrapped around who everyone is from the men, to their women and the babies that don't seem to stop coming. Oh, so many babies!" Horace kidded.

"Right. Marlow and I are loving Maia with everything in us. I never saw myself as a father. It never occurred to me that I would be one. Now that I am, both a father and a husband, I can't see my life being anything else. What about you? Is there a significant other? I know you're the consummate workaholic and bachelor, but surely there is someone."

Horace shook his head.

"Not at the moment. I've never seen myself as the relationship type of guy. Life in Vegas is a lot different than here in Chicago. It's not called *sin city* for nothing. There is a lot of sinning happening there around the clock. That place can become addictive with all of those beautiful women. It's a man's and a woman's playground. Most of my adult life, that's where I've lived after college. I have some stories I could tell you about being knee deep in the sinning part of life there. I needed this break."

"You mean no one has captured your heart? That's crazy!"

"I keep things casual. Besides, work has always been the priority. Torrence and I worked our asses off to get that casino up and running in Vegas. From there, we're now on our third location. I'm still trying to figure out how he was able to do it with Reese and now with the baby."

"Perhaps, one day for you? You know it's possible to gamble with love and win. Before I met Marlow, I was connected to a lot of beauties. That includes one of the hottest female wrappers in the country – possibly in the world. She was wild; as wild as I was. The day Marlow crashed into my car with her car, that was the start of the best days of my life. I know it sounds foolish because the accident was a bad one. Still, I don't know if I would have been as focused on my career and life as I am now if it hadn't been for her. I now have her and my daughter to take care of. That gives me a reason to give wrestling my all."

"Is Marlow still working or planning to go back to work after Maia is older?"

Horace thought back to his own mother who tried to juggle working and raising two boys. Now, she's raising two teenage girls, his sisters. He still struggles with not having a relationship with them, though he would like one beyond the texting they do back and forth. Life is different for him.

"She's planning on going back to work but not full-time until Maia is in school. She wants to be a very hands-on mother. We're already talking about having a second child."

"Joey, that's amazing! It's good to see."

"Like, I said, one day for you too, I'm sure."

"We'll see about that. How are things going with your sister-in-law, Angel. I know it's been a few days. I've been crazy busy and haven't had a chance to catch with how things are going? Is she out?"

"Oh, yeah, she's out. She had her initial court date and was released on her own recognizance. She's staying with Marlow and me. She has another court date, though I'm not sure of the date. Up next is an emergency family court date tomorrow. It was supposed to be the day after Angel got out, but the judge had an emergency. Angel's lawyer was going to request another judge, but a friend in her law firm told her she will want to stick with the first judge, who is more lenient than some of the other options. Angel agreed to wait, though she was sad that it meant that she couldn't see her daughter yet. Marlow and I are trying to get temporary custody of Marleigh, that's Angel's daughter."

"She's still in the system?" Horace questioned.

The idea of that rubbed him the wrong way. He couldn't imagine what Angel must be going through not having her baby with her.

"She is and we're trying to remedy that. Angel is devastated, especially since they won't let her see Marleigh in-person. When they let her out of jail, she slept for two straight days. She scared Marlow, who wouldn't sleep either. She kept thinking she would wake up and Angel would have skipped out again."

"Did she?" Horace asked, hoping that didn't happen.

"No, she stayed put. She really wants her baby back. If she goes anywhere, it won't be until she gets Marleigh back. Even then, I think she wants to stay around. Marlow and her brother Steven have been close to Angel. They finally told their mother what happened. She came by last night. It's a good thing I was home. Delores, their mother, and Marlow go at each other something terrible. When it got to be too stressful, I had Steven take Delores home. She's a handful. Angel is doing good though. She just cries a lot. For now, we have her in our guest bedroom, so Marlow hears every cry and every wail that comes out of Angel when she's alone and missing her baby."

"So, what's the plan that you and Marlow are trying to put in place? Can I help in any way?"

"We're not sure if we'll be able to get Marleigh tomorrow. If we can't we are hoping to get the chance to set eyes on her other than via pictures or video. Thankfully, the temporary foster family is good with sending pictures and all so that Angel can make it through the day. That little girl is so gorgeous. You can tell she and Maia are related. They could almost be twins."

"Does Kris think things will go your way?"

"She thinks we have a better chance of getting temporary custody over Angel getting her back right now. If we can get that far, Angel will be living with us, if the court is okay with that, and she'll get to be with Marleigh every day. Kris thinks that the lawyer representing child services will recommend foster care until Angel's misdemeanor criminal case is over. The issue of assaulting an officer is what's actually hurting her the most. I get it. She saw her baby being taken and she lost it. I would have done the same if I saw someone taking Maia away. Marlow would have too. We don't know how long that whole situation will be so we're fighting that. We'll find out tomorrow. I'm glad it's coming up soon because in a few days, I'll be heading out of town for a match that I've already signed the contract for in Miami. So much is going on. I feel like I'm on roller skates with all of this."

"Joey, how can I help? What can I do?"

Horace watched the wheels turning in Joey's head. He was probably wondering why he kept offering to help when he doesn't even know Angel or even Marlow that well. He didn't want to say that he felt a connection to Angel's struggles. He's had his own struggles in life.

"Are you serious about helping? Do you have the time? I don't want to put too much on you."

"Joey, I'm here. Tell me what you need," Horace pushed.

"I hate to be crazy worried about Marlow and Angel while I'm out of town. Carlos said he would help but he and Everly have their own baby. Everyone seems to have a lot of focuses which is understandable. I think if we can show that Angel is serious about doing the right thing for herself and Marleigh that the judge would be open to giving her a chance, especially with her staying with us."

"I'm holding out hope for a good outcome."

"Thanks, Horace. I appreciate you for that. We have a lower level at the house that Marlow wants to turn into a small apartment for Angel. That way, she can have her own space. It's mostly storage. It has a full bathroom and two rooms that could be turned into bedrooms, one for Angel and one for Marleigh. There is a large living space and a nice size kitchen. It also has its own entrance from the outside. You've been to my house. There are steps that lead up and another set that lead down. The lower level needs some work. Marlow is going to get some furniture for the living space, bedroom furniture for Angel and baby stuff for Marleigh for the second bedroom. If we get the okay, we'll need to move quickly. Can you recommend someone to help with the minor fixes? It really needs a fresh coat of paint, a new entry door with new locks and a separate alarm system. There are other things that Marlow has noted. Of course, she wants to do it all now. She wants Angel to feel like it can be a place where she belongs; where she can begin to rebuild her life. Did I mention that her drug test came back clean? The woman who said she saw Angel doing heavy drugs days ago actually lied. In fact, we believe the cop lied as well. He's someone who was trying to take advantage of Angel in a sexual way. When she thwarted his advances and threatened to tell his wife, that's when things went left. He set her up to lose her baby. It has to all be sorted out, and it will. In the meantime, having a place Angel can call home is the priority. If I didn't have this match, I would be all over this."

"I got it. Don't worry about a thing. Tell Marlow I'll be over and we can talk about what needs to be done. I'm actually pretty handy myself. If there is a big job, yeah, I've got people. If it's just minor fixes, I can handle those. I want to help."

"Bro, in the midst of all that you have going on with the casino opening, you think you have time to help us out? I mean, I appreciate it if you can, but I don't want to put you out knowing what's ahead of you for opening day."

"Well, Torrence and I already have our new managers on the books and working. They'll be four of them at the new casino. You met Cliff today. The other three are around here somewhere. They can more than handle the day to day of making sure equipment and things are delivered and set up. I'm learning to delegate more anyway. Let me help. You don't need to be worried about anything. I don't want Carlos to worry either when I know he and Everly are new parents. He's also working on the new security team being setup. I'm the only one in our circle without a wife and kids, so time is something I have. Why don't we talk before you head out of town. You can run everything by me, including giving me a tour of the lower level. Plus, I'm planning on being at family court to support you, Marlow and Angel tomorrow. One thing

I do know from back when Torrence and his family took me in is that, having people there with you in court as support looks good to any judge. Whatever you and your family need, let me know."

"If you're sure, I don't know how to say thank you enough. I know Torrence, my brother and my brother-in-law and their wives will be around to help Marlow. Having you around to support as well would be magnificent. I think that would make Marlow feel better knowing that the repairs would get done. It's the first step in what we'll be able to tell the family court judge tomorrow. Now, with the little time we have left to chat, let's talk about a few celebrities I was able to secure for the casino opening events. Remember I told you about the female wrapper I was involved with?"

"Micki Sunaj?" Horace asked.

"Yes, that's her. With Marlow's blessing, after knowing about my *fun times* with her, I've asked her about performing and she said anything for me and Marlow. She's actually happy for us. I've got a few more top-tier celebrities that will knock your socks off."

Joey reached into his pocket for his phone and texted him the list of names that quickly said yes.

"Oh, yeah, this list is hot! It's a good thing I've reserved several of our best suites for special guests. Let me get my iPad out of my bag. I need to email this to myself. I'll tell you who I have confirmed already. I'll get my assistant in here to work on getting contracts signed and suites secured. That night will be epic!" Horace declared.

"You and Torrence have a gift with all of this. I'm just happy to be a part."

Horace stood to grab his iPad as his thoughts turned to Angel, whom he has yet to meet. That didn't matter to him. He felt good knowing that if he could play even a small part in helping Angel get back up on her feet, he was all over it.

4

Angel sat on the hard wooden bench in the courtroom more nervous than she has ever been. This isn't her first time in some sort of trouble. This wasn't even her first time in family court. There was a time after she had her son that she'd been arrested for drug use. She had Angelo with her that day. She didn't get arrested but she did get a date to come to court to prove that she and Santiago could properly look after their son.

After Angelo died, it was deemed an accident. That happened in Florida and wasn't pursued by law enforcement, to her bewilderment. She just knew she was going to jail. She discovered no action would be taken after it was noted that the gate to the pool was broken. That allowed Angelo to get through it and to the pool. After that all went down, she decided to not go home ever again and disappeared. She slept here, there and everywhere. That's when her struggle in life began all over again. She hated that she couldn't catch a break. It was her own fault. She should have called Marlow a long time ago.

Looking around and behind her, Angel was surprised to see so many people in the courtroom. She wondered if they were all there for her. She got her answer when each person hugged Marlow and Joey. As her lawyer continued talking to her, she couldn't take her eyes off of the ten to twelve people who sat in the back of the courtroom. She leaned over to her attorney to inquire.

"Who are all of those people? My sister said her husband, his brother and his brother's wife would be here. I see my brother and my mother. Who are the rest of the people?" she asked.

"Let me see. First there is Joey's sister, Alyssa and her husband Dexter. Then there is Carter and Sienna Garrison. They are friends too. Then Torrence and Reese. Next to Torrence is his best friend, Horace. I know him because he's the friend of my brother that got me here as your attorney. If it weren't for him, I assume you have someone else representing you."

Angel perked up.

"Oh, that's him? Marlow told me about him. I will have to make sure and thank him. You're doing a great job. Marlow thinks we have a good chance of her and Joey getting Marleigh temporarily."

"That's what I'll be fighting for today. It's still an up-hill battle, but I'm ready for it. Oh, I forgot to tell you that the last couple is our esteemed mayor and his wife Nichelle. As you can see, she's about to have a baby any day now. They are all here to support not just your sister and Joey, but you and Marleigh. They wanted to show a wall of support in front of the judge so that we can prove that you have some really great people in your corner. Carter and Dexter own the top luxury car dealerships in Chicago along with other multi-million-dollar businesses. Torrence and Horace own three casinos, including one that is on the cusp of opening up soon. Reese owns a lucrative marketing firm and Sienna owns her own dental practice. She just opened up her second location."

"Whew, my sister has a super group of powerful friends," Angel said.

Kris leaned over close to her and smiled.

"And now, so do you. Embrace it. These people are the best chance you have of getting your daughter back even if it's through your sister. At least, you'll be in the same home as your daughter. There will be restrictions. Make sure you agree to them all; not just some, but every single one of them. Even if it feels like you don't have many rights at this time, go along with what I'm going to recommend. It's the best for now. I know I sound like I'm repeating myself when I say this again and again, but I need to be sure you understand the importance of keeping your cool. Are you good with that?" Kris asked her.

Angel was willing to give up a limb if it meant she got to have Marleigh back. She trusted Marlow and had no problem agreeing to giving her temporary custody.

"All rise."

Angel looked up as the judge and a few other people entered the courtroom. When she looked to the left, there were two ladies on the table opposite her and Kris. She turned and locked eyes with her sister for support. Marlow gave her two-thumbs up. That made Angel feel better. She turned and sat when the judge asked them to all have a seat. She hoped that her mother, who was also there, would not speak and interrupt. Keeping Delores quiet was going to be a huge task.

Already, before they entered the courtroom, she was in the hall with her mother and brother. Her mother was getting loud when she questioned why Marlow's house is where she chose to live instead of coming home with her. Steven interrupted and spoke up to remind their mother of the current man living in her house. If the representatives from child services did a visit to the house to see if it was a place for Marleigh to be, she would never get custody. Between all the alcohol and cigarette butts everywhere, they wouldn't let an adult move in there. Angel started to laugh when Steven said all that, but she held it in. Besides, the only person that she could think of that any court would allow her daughter to go home with is Marlow. She was counting on that happening today. Knowing her baby is in the system kept her up crying night after night since she got out of jail. She needed her back. Marleigh made her whole for the first time in a long time.

When Marlow finally walked over to them and put their mother in her place, her mother finally quieted. Marlow warned her to either be quiet or don't come inside the courtroom. She was serious that there be no drama when the placement of her niece was on the line.

Turning her attention back to what was happening in the courtroom, Angel listened as the woman from the other table talked about how Marleigh was better off in foster care where she is now until Angel could get her life back on track. They believe it will take some time for her to do that and they don't want to risk Marleigh being in an unstable environment. Angel had to force her lips to stay closed. She couldn't ruin her own case when the other side painted her as some kind of unfit mother. They brought up her current legal problems and the fact that until she was released from jail, she wasn't going to have a place to stay. They claim to still not know what her plans were for where she would live and how she could possibly take care of herself and a baby who would need a lot of love, care and attention.

Angel sat with her legs shaking nervously in the black dress pants and white top that Marlow had bought for her to wear. Her hands gripped the wooden seat of each side of her body. She heard the words and forced herself to tune them out. Most of what they spoke were lies. Still, she did as her lawyer advised. She remained silent. Then it was Kris' turn to speak. That's when Angel tuned back in to the proceedings.

"Your honor, first let me say that I appreciate that my colleagues on the other side of the room have done a great job of temporarily placing Marleigh with a nice, gracious family who have been sending pictures and videos of Marleigh to her mother and her family. They love that she is being cared for in an amazing way. I would like to counter some of the things that have been said about my client today. I know that this is family court and I'm not speaking in reference to a criminal case. Ms. Angel Reagan has had her struggles in life. She's tried her best to make amends for the things that she's done that have tarnished her name. Yes, she lost a child to a drowning that was declared an accident. Ms. Reagan was never charged with anything drug related in that accident. My colleagues in the law should not have brought those assumptions up about her child, Angelo passing away due to her drug habit. I don't have any court records that state that. I would like that information stricken. I would also like to counter the idea that Ms. Reagan isn't stable enough to have her daughter back yet. Yes, there is a pending court case of a criminal nature. Charges have been filed but no guilt has been declared. I would also like to point out that Ms. Reagan has a large gathering of supporters with her in court today to show that they will help her in any way they can to get back up on her feet. Her main goal is to become a productive member of society. I do not agree that it's in the best interest of her daughter to be away from her mother when it's clear that there are other alternatives. One being that Ms. Reagan's sister, Marlow and her husband, Joseph Kincaid are here and have agreed to accept temporary custody of Marleigh into their home. Mrs. Kincaid is a licensed physical therapist who has had extensive training in the medical field. They also have an infant daughter of their own. Marleigh would fit right in since Mrs. Kincaid is currently on extended maternity leave. We all know who Mr. Joseph Kincaid is," Kris added.

"Yes. It's good to see you Mr. Kincaid. I've been a fan of your career from the start," the judge said.

"Thank you, sir," Joey responded.

"Judge, we also have our very own mayor of Chicago, the honorable Tucker Glass and his wife here today."

"Judge Keto, it's good to see you again," Tucker said from the rear.

"Mayor Glass. The feeling is mutual. Good see you too."

"We also have the owners of the city's newest casino and one to soon open, here with us today, Torrence Allen and Horace Grant. I introduce all of them to say that Ms. Reagan has a better chance than she's ever had to get on the right path with all of these people in her corner. If you would like, they could each attest that they will be there for her and baby Marleigh. Now, we are not requesting that the baby be handed over to Ms. Reagan right away. I do believe they should be able to continue their bond, with oversight, of course."

Kris looked to her and Angel nodded her head.

"You are correct that I will not turn the baby back over to Ms. Reagan at this time."

Angel knew there was a plan. She remained patient.

"Yes, sir. We understand that. There is ample space at the Kincaid home. They even have a lower level that is being turned into a two-bedroom apartment. What we don't want is to keep Marleigh away from her mother for any long period of time. The mother-daughter bond is a special one. As you can see from the report in your copy of the file, that Ms. Reagan's drug test came back absolutely clean. There was no trace of any type of drug, not even aspirin, in her system. That case, of course will be held in court in the coming weeks. All we ask is that the court would allow Ms. Reagan's family to support her efforts to get on the straight and narrow. Her brother and her mother are also here today and offer their help with anything she needs, especially when it comes to the welfare of the baby. As you can see, this kind of support here for her today is unprecedented. Powerful businessman, the mayor, entertainers and family. They are all here. We only ask that you not continue to allow the system to break yet another family up without any real claims that can be substantiated. Thank you."

Once Kris sat down, Angel patted her on the leg and whispered thank you. The courtroom was silent as the judge spent some time writing some things down.

"What's happening?" Angel asked Kris.

"We're waiting for his ruling. Give him a few minutes. He's probably writing down those stipulations I told you about. This time of silence is a good thing. If he was going to say no to our option, he could have done that immediately. I've seen this before. I think we're in a good place. Let's wait it out."

Angel nodded and turned to look back at everyone seated in the back behind them. As her eyes went down the row, there was a set of eyes that called out to her. She couldn't look away. She saw in those eyes a sense of peace that she'd never seen before. When he smiled at her, for some reason, her existence felt at ease. When he winked at her, she smiled and turned back around. What was that? Besides the fact that he was drop-dead gorgeous, he actually winked at her. The wink and his smile put her at ease for the first time today. A warmth radiated from him to her. She sat up straight and was ready for this next phase of her life if the judge was willing to take a chance on her.

"Ms. Reagan, today is going to be your lucky day. I'm not sure how many times someone has given you grace, but today, I'm going to do just that. I can't give you sole custody of your daughter back as of yet. I will, however, grant temporary custody to Mr. and Mrs. Joseph and Marlow Kincaid. For the next sixty-days, they will have responsibility for Marleigh Shiloh Reagan, age nine-months old. They will maintain custody in their home where you will also reside. You must get weekly counseling for the next six-months. I know that your last drug test came back clean. You must also agree to random drug tests for the next sixty days. If there is any question about those test results, you will not be allowed to remain in the same residence as your daughter. Either she will have to be placed back with a foster family or you would need to find another place to live. Is that understood?" the judge asked.

Angel looked to Kris who gave her the green light to respond.

"Yes, I understand," she acknowledged.

"I expect you to either get into a program that will help you seek employment, go to school or if you already have employment, the court will need information on that. If that's the case, please be mindful of our surrounding. It will all have an impact on whether your daughter stays where you will be around her every day. You need to be productive to take care of your daughter. I have no doubt that where you will both be staying, you will have the chance to succeed with their help and support. It's wonderful that you have this big group of people behind you. Not many people have a fourth of what that group represents. There will be visits by child services. They will be scheduled. Until we reconvene here in two months, you cannot be left alone in the home with your daughter, though you can reside with her in the part of the house that your sister is establishing for you. I am in agreement with that. I am providing you with a list of counselors or you can pick one of your own that the court must approve. I am adding the next court date to my calendar. That information will be shared with you. I would like for those who are here today representing the minor child to have a chance to see the residence where you and your daughter will be living. The court will agree to a visit within a week. I have no doubt that the living arrangements will be sufficient. Still, I must have the information on the visit on file. The court will wait to see what comes out of your other court cast that is currently pending in the district court. Ms. Devereaux? Is the minor child here at the courthouse right now?" the judge asked.

Angel looked over when she stood up behind the light brown wood desk.

"Yes, judge. She is in one of the waiting rooms."

"Ms. Reagan, do you have any questions for the court at this time? I want to be sure that I'm giving you enough time to have all of your questions answered and understood."

Angel shook her head no and then realized the judge was waiting for her to speak. She stood up after getting nudged by Kris.

"No, sir. I do want to thank you for giving me another chance to get my life right. I promise to follow everything you said I must do and much more. All I want is to be able to see my daughter every day. To hold her and love on her is my priority."

"That's what I like to hear. Unless there are other questions, that is the order of this court. Ms. Devereaux, please complete the paperwork and hand the minor child over to Mr. and Mrs. Joseph Kincaid. Good luck to you, Ms. Reagan. I hope to see you soon where I can give full custody back to you."

Angel smiled. She was so happy, she wanted to run, jump and dance.

"Thank you."

When the judge stood and left, Angel raced to the back of the room and was surrounded in a big hug by her sister, brother and mother.

"We did it!" Marlow declared.

"Yes! Can we go get Marleigh now?" Angel questioned.

She turned to Kris when she walked up.

"Ms. Devereaux is on her way to have Marleigh brought in. It's going to be about thirty minutes. There are clearances she has to make. Marlow, did you all bring a car seat?"

"Yes!" Marlow and Joey declared together, causing everyone to laugh.

As others left the courtroom after wishing her well, Angel noticed one person, besides Marlow and Stephen stayed behind. He walked up to her. Angel turned her whole body around and faced him. She thought he was handsome when she saw him from a distance. Now being this close, she'd never seen a more gorgeous specimen of a man in her life. He was tall, over six-feet, dark skin like chocolate lava. His attire of all black from his button-down shirt under his back suit jacket with blue denims and black dress shoes to his shiny gold watch on one wrist to the thick gold bracelet chain on his other arm had the man looking live he should be on a magazine cover.

"Hello, I'm Horace. I just want to say I'm glad things turned out in your favor. I was hoping they would."

Angel held her hand out for him to shake while her eyes never left his.

"Thank you for helping me. Kris told me that you're the one who got her to represent me by way of her brother. Without her, I'm not sure I would have been this lucky. Thanks for being in the room as part of my support team today. I appreciate it."

"You'll see me around. I'm going to work on the few updates to the apartment for you and your daughter. Until that's done, Marlow said you'll be staying upstairs in the main part of the house. I'm glad I could help in any way."

"Oh, okay. Then I guess I'll see you around the house."

When they finally let go of each other hands, Angel noticed something about the way he was gazing at her. She was intrigued. She hoped he was too.

"Yes, you will."

When he turned to leave, Angel stood in place and watched him until he was out of sight.

"Whew, that's a man, right?" Kris asked.

Angel turned to her.

"You like him?" Angel asked.

"Honey? Are you serious? The way that man was gazing at you, I would say he doesn't have eyes for anyone but you. I say go for it. Gorgeous and established? Oh, did I mention that he's single?"

Angel smiled.

"Is he?"

"Only one way to find out. Besides, he'll be around the house. Now, let's go get your baby. I bet she has missed you as much as you have missed her."

"That's for damn sure!" Angel cheered as they left the courtroom.

It wasn't lost on her that once in the hallway, she looked for Horace. The moment they locked eyes yet again, she silently hoped that he was single. Not that she was ready for another man at this time considering she needed to focus on Marleigh, but it didn't hurt to look. Looking is exactly what she was doing. Funny thing was, so was he; right at her.

"Get a room already," Steven whispered in her ear.

His sudden appearance made her jump. She wondered if anyone else had caught her staring at Horace.

"What are you talking about?" she asked him when he linked his arm with hers and headed toward the room where Marleigh was waiting for them.

"You and the new guy? There is something there. Oh, I'm not just talking about you. When a man looks at a woman the way he was at you, he's serious. He's not one of those play things you've been dealing with in the past."

Angel didn't respond. She turned her head one last time. She hoped to find him still looking her way. She smiled when her wish was granted. Today was her lucky day indeed.

5

"Alright everybody, listen up."

Horace looked at his watch for the tenth time in the past hour during the meeting with the four casino managers. His plan was to already be out of the office and over to Marlow's house to finish the work he'd begun a week ago after she and Joey were granted temporary custody of Angel's daughter. With Joey out of town, he'd also been helping Carlos look in on Marlow. So far, there hadn't been any issues other than the updates to the house.

Today, the new entry door to the lower-level apartment was being delivered. He had about an hour before the crew he'd hired to pick up the door would arrive at the house. Besides that, he had also ordered a new vanity and toilet for the bathroom that he'd painted the day before. After speaking with Angel a few times throughout the week, he'd found out that she loved the color yellow. He'd found a nice golden yellow at the paint store.

All week, he'd gone between his work at the casino office and working on Marlow's house. Truth be told, he barely had time to eat or sleep, but he made it through with extra coffee. He was determined to make sure that if he could prevent Angel from going through any stress beyond what she's already going through, he would do it. They had become pretty good friends in a week's time.

"Horace? You were saying?" Cliff asked.

All heads turned when Torrence entered the office and closed the door behind him. He waved and stayed near the door. Horace nodded in his direction.

"Sorry guys. I was distracted there for a moment. I was trying to say that we're still a few months out from the grand opening. I looked at all the equipment and furniture that's been set up and everything looks good. The machines need to be checked and rechecked quite a few times before we open. We've got a lot done. There is more to do. I know I've been missing in action a bit this past week. Thanks to Torrence who has been making himself more of a presence. Of course, it goes without saying that I appreciate each of you for stepping in early and making sure everything is going smoothly."

"You know we've got your back; you and Torrence. We know you have your hands full helping out a friend. Keep doing what you're doing. We've got the casino covered," Cliff said. The other men nodded their agreement.

"I appreciate that. I'm always available even when you don't see me around here. Torrence, anything from you before these guys head out?" Horace asked.

"Nothing for them. I do have a few questions for you about the executive office staff that we still need to hire. We can do that when you're finished here."

"Cool. I'll be leaving in about thirty minutes, so if you need something, let me know before I'm out."

The managers left out leaving him and Torrence alone.

"I don't want to tie up your time because I know you have someplace to be. I stopped by to see if there was anything I could do to help around here. Reese and the baby are out with her sister. I just left the other casino and things are on track for tonight's comedy tour kickoff. As usual, along the lines with other events, every show for every night has already been sold out. All the hotel rooms are booked. I left the team to handle things so that I could check out what was happening around here. Looking good, bro. You've done a great job. Did I ever say how glad I am that you agreed to come here and take over oversight of the new casino? I don't know what I would do without you. The issues Reese had with her pregnancy had me scared. You stepped in right on time."

"That was an easy, yes. You know all you have to do is send out the bat signal and I'm there, wherever and whenever you need."

"It's been that way from the very beginning. Do you remember how we started out as rivals on two different basketball teams and quickly became friends?" Torrence asked.

Horace leaned back in his office chair as he tapped a pen on his desk, remembering a time long ago when they were teenagers.

"That was a long time ago. Can you believe it's been seventeen years or so? That same year, I left home, or what the system called running away, I thought I would be living on the streets as a sixteen-year-old. If it hadn't been for your parents helping me talk my parents into allowing me to become an emancipated minor, I don't know where life would have taken me. All I knew was that I couldn't go back to that house where my brother and I lived under my father's hard rules. My grades were terrible. My attitude was even worse. My life didn't seem clear until your parents took me in. Look at us now. I miss my brother but this is where I was supposed to be at this time in my life because of you. "

"We started at the bottom and now we're here," he declared, raising his hand far above his head.

"Life is good. I see life and love is good to you. Reese really did a job on you. She tamed that wild beast that was you when we lived in Vegas. I like this side of you; the family man. The businessman has always been in you. I never thought I'd see the day."

"I'm still waiting on that day for you. In the meantime, so that you can get on your way, when are the interviews going to start for the administrative staff. You mentioned you wanted them in place at least two months before we open. I know we have some temporary staff fielding calls and such. I didn't know if you wanted me to handle the last of the staff that we need to hire. The hiring agency you went with did a great job on all of the other staff, especially the hotel and restaurant staff. We're still waiting on the security clearance of the casino staff. Carlos' security firm is wrapping up all those background checks. He told me last night that all the new hires for casino and hotel security are good to go. I sent you the dossier on all of them. The last is our own staff in the front office. Where are we with that?"

Horace had a plan for that.

"I'm bringing a few people from our administrative staff in Vegas to oversee the hiring of the staff here. First choice will go to anyone from the temporary staff who wants to stay on permanently. I have it covered, though my life is a bit crazy right now. I don't want you to worry about that."

"Okay, I see you superman. I will leave that to you and back off. And Angel? How is she? I talked with Marlow but we didn't get a chance to talk about Angel other than that she loves the upgrades you and your team have done. Where did you get those guys? I may need a few things done at my house."

"Outside of a home improvement retail store that I go to all the time. You know I did my own upgrades to my apartment at the casino here and in Las Vegas."

"You've always been good with your hands. My mom still raves about those shelves in her craft room that you built."

"I learned from guys like the ones I find who help me here and there. Listen, those guys know their stuff. The things I need an extra hand for, they are always on top of. The place looks amazing. As for Angel, she's good."

Horace looked away from Torrence and focused on the gold door knob to his office, for no reason at all.

Torrence chuckled and Horace looked back at him.

"That's it? That's all I get is, she's good? She's beautiful."

"Bro!!!!!!!!!!" Horace yelled.

"Don't, bro, me. I know that look You like her."

Horace let out a loud sigh.

"She is beyond beautiful. I haven't acted on anything. She's not like the typical woman for me."

"Oh? What does that mean? She's gorgeous inside and out; especially out. She is definitely your type. What? Is it that she has a kid? I have noticed that in all of the women I've known you to be connected to over the years, not one of them has had any kids. It's like you're allergic to them or something."

"Man, don't label me like that. I see what you're saying, but that's not the case here. Single women without kids have always been easier because of what I was engaging in with them. Some single women with kids are interested in finding a man who is looking to settle down. That wasn't me."

When Torrence lifted one eye-brow in a questionable fashion, Horace knew what he'd said wrong. Before he could correct himself, Torrence spoke up first.

"*Wasn't?* Do you mean that is you now? Is that because of Angel? Does she have you under some spell?" Torrence joked.

"I bet you see how Reese got me out of those streets and other women's beds," Torrence joked.

Horace heard the humor in his question but felt a sense of reality in his own thoughts.

"You know what I mean. Vegas is different from Chicago. Joey and I were recently talking about that. You are right about one thing – I do like Angel. As for her daughter, that little girl has me all wrapped up. When I'm there and Angel comes downstairs with her or I go up if they're in the kitchen, Marleigh's eyes land on me and she's all smiles. Playing with her is as natural as breathing. When I leave there and go home to my oneness existence, I realize that I've been so busy having fun that I've forgotten to actually live."

"But Ace? What about her? The two of you were pretty close in Vegas. Through my connections in Vegas, I hear that she's completely spent over you. You're not interested in anything other than burning up the sheets?"

"No, not even in the least. I like Ace. She's a barrel of fun, but there is no future there. I think she's leaning toward that. Do you know that she, her sister and both of her brothers are all single? Not one relationship or marriage in the bunch and Ace is the youngest of them at thirty-one. I think she likes playing the streets just as much as a man. Besides, her gambling habits are a bit much for me. She stays in trouble when it comes to her finances. She's fun but there is no future there. I'm thinking more about the future and what that looks like for me. I see more in it. I see a much slower, yet still exciting life. Ace is Vegas and what that city stands for. I see the difference and I'm not Vegas anymore. Yes, we have the casino there, but my life can't be Vegas anymore. That's something I wanted to talk to you about. What do you say to me staying in Chicago after the casino opens? I know we talked about six months or so and then I'd head back to Vegas. I'd like a change. Thoughts?"

Horace had been thinking about making Chicago a permanent home for himself for some time now; before he met Angel. Though after just one week of getting to know her, he wanted to know more. He wanted to spend more time with her. Through their talks, she has made him reconsider being involved with just one woman. Never has been him, but could very much be him if he discovered she liked him as much as he liked her.

"Horace, you are the one who said you would come to Chicago and handle business but that you were going to hightail it back to Vegas on the first thing smoking after the casino opened. That was why we hired the four new managers to help me run this place along with the six managers at our West location. I have been pushing you about staff hiring because in my head, I was preparing for you leaving Chicago in less than a year. If you love Chicago and really want my two cents, yes, stay in Chicago and run this place. You've been here a while now and look how smoothly the casino in Vegas is running. Profits are still through the roof. The concert venue has comedic and music artist residencies through the next five years. We're already reviewing contracts for more events for now and years down the road for that location. We have the best team running that place. You and I have both flown there several times in the past few months and there hasn't been one issue. That's saying a lot for Las Vegas. The night club has a sold out crowd every night of the week. We can't ask for more than that other than for the two casinos and hotels here in Chicago to do the same and become as successful. We can do that with us both being here in Chicago. Besides, Carter, Dexter and Carlos want to talk to us about a joint business venture. Those guys are thinking beyond the stars and I think we should sit down with them to talk about it."

The excitement that flew through is body could barely be contained. Horace was more than up for that.

"Hell yeah! Let's do that. You know I'm not a flashy guy when it comes to cars, jewelry, etc., but I am interested in anything that would make me more money. Who is setting that up?" he asked.

"I think we'll hear from Carter soon. He's off to Miami, I think, in reference to a new dealership he and Dexter are planning on opening up there. Can you believe those dudes are opening yet another dealership? We are all seeing the worth in expanding to other states."

"Joey is there right now," Horace added.

"I heard. Carter said he was going to the wrestling match while he's there. I'm sure we'll hear something soon. I think he wanted to wait until after the opening of the casino and hotel. I told him if he wanted to do it sooner, we would accommodate that. You down?"

"I sure am. Let's do it. Before you leave, I want you to know that we received an RSVP from Rihanna and ASAP Rocky. They're doing it as a favor to Joey, whom they are both good friends with. He's also going to be a special guest model for her new men's line of boxer briefs."

"Yes! I was hoping that was the case. The modeling thing though? Interesting change for him. They will be a big draw. You know she's my hall pass, right?" Torrence joked.

"Don't let me pick up the phone and call Reese and snitch on you," Horace quipped.

"Trust me, she knows my love for everything Rihanna. We both have that one hall pass person."

"Oh?" Horace was intrigued. "Who is hers?"

"Some new guy on the seen named Aaron Pierre. He plays Mufasa in the latest Lion King movie. I try not to get too into it. We were having fun with it one night and asked each other. It's all good and healthy conversation. Besides, the Fenty Lingerie line gets all of my money. My sexy wife loves that stuff! Listen, I can see you in love, married with a bunch of kids. I know you never saw that for yourself because of your childhood. I want you to give yourself some grace. You are always the person who extends help and grace to everyone else but you never take care of your own self in the same way. Your past is what it is. After you moved in with us, I learned a lot about what life was like for you growing up. Your father was and probably still is a terrible man. I hope he has softened up after he and your mother had your sisters. What are they like fifteen and sixteen now?"

"Yeah. Liza is fifteen and Lisa is sixteen; both are in high school. I haven't talked to them in a month. I need to check in on them. I send them money regularly. I've also set up bank accounts and education accounts for them for college. I don't' want them stuck in North Carolina. I want them to see and experience the world. Did I tell you that my parents are divorced?"

"Wow! Really? Since when?"

Horace was as surprised as Torrence is right now when he first heard. His sister Liza snuck in a phone call to him one day. She confessed to him that their mother finally stood up against him and kicked him out. She saw that he was trying to be the strong arm of the law with his sisters and his mother had suffered enough. She wasn't having it for her daughters. That was something he was happy to hear. What his father took him and his brother through no one knew but Torrence. He'd never told another living soul.

"About six months. When Liza last called, that's what she wanted me to know. Each month I text to keep up. She also begged me to come visit them; at least her and Lisa. We talk via facetime, but I have never seen my sisters in person."

"Before you question yourself, go see them. Do not let your history with your father and mother taint your relationship with your sisters. They need their big brother. The only reason I am a big brother is because of you. My mother couldn't have any more children. She was happy when you came to live with us. I bet if we put our phones down and each called her at the same time then hung up, you would be the first one she would call back."

Horace laughed out loud.

"That's because she's always worried about me more than you. I'll think about going to see my sisters. It's been a lot of years. More like seventeen. My mother was pregnant when I left. I don't know. I'm starting to see life different. I think all of this stuff with Angel has brought out something in me that makes me want to face my demons. Angel is twenty-five but has lived a lifetime it seems. She's trying to find herself just like I still am. We're alike in a lot of ways. I'm drawn to her, not just because of that, but because I enjoy talking to her. She and Marlow made me dinner the other night and I felt seen and heard if a different way."

"You've fallen for Angel. Is it the damsel in the distress thing?" Torrence inquired.

Horace wondered that himself, at first. Then he realized he simply enjoyed being around her and her daughter. He loved that he could make her smile just by giving her an update on her apartment. She allowed him to winddown and think about things other than work. The other night, they spent hours talking about their love for old movies. They both love the original Sparkle and Cooley High. Who couldn't love that movie? After today's final updates on the apartment, he'll be close to finishing.

"Not at all. I checked myself on that just to be sure. I like her, Torrence. I mean, I really like her. I don't have to *be 'sin city'* Horace around her. I can put away the high-life Horace. I can just be Horace Grant, the man who is working with his hands to better her life."

Torrence stood to leave. Horace stood with him.

"Get out of here and get to the house. I like this new Horace. I want him to spend even more time with Angel. You're good for each other. I'll wrap up things around this place before I leave. I'm going to head back over to the other casino before meeting my wife and daughter for dinner. You good?"

Horace nodded. He was better than that.

"In about twenty minutes when I get to the house and set my eyes on Angel, I'll be great!"

6

Angel sat in the bay window on the plush burnt orange seat that allowed her to see up and down their Chicago neighborhood street. People walked about with their pets and some with babies in strollers. She and Marlow had just gotten in from taking Marleigh and Maia out for a walk since it was a nice, warm day. Now that they were back, Marleigh was in her arms, quickly falling asleep after a full bottle and a plate of veggies and her favorite, strawberries.

She was enjoying how life has finally slowed down for her. Being back in Chicago and with her family was exactly what she and Marleigh needed in their lives. This first full week of finally having Marleigh back was nothing short of a miracle. She only had bleak thoughts after she was arrested. Without being on drugs, she was looking at life differently.

When Marleigh started to fuss, she lifted her up and placed her head on her shoulder. She has learned that her daughter loves being in that position. Angel didn't care what position her baby loved being in, she would put her in a million of them as long as she could hold her like this all the time.

"She's going to get used to that," Marlow said walking up.

Angel grinned knowing that her sister was right. She couldn't help it. Being away from her for those few days was torturous.

"I know. You keep saying that. I'm just so thankful that she's with us; well, with you and Joey. I love her feel. I love her smell. Her chunky little fingers are so cute. I need to have her close. I could have lost her. They took my custody away."

"No, Angel. Don't do that. Marleigh is with you, her mother. I don't care what the court says. We are following all of their rules, but you are her mother and you are the one caring for her. I'm just here overseeing because the court says that I must do that. I can't speak for them, but I have all faith in you as her mother. I know you're doing and will continue to do the right thing. I don't walk around here with my eye on you every second of every day. Be a mother. If you need me, I'm here. That's why I'm here. Besides, she loves you so much."

"Just as much as I love her. I wish she'd had the chance to meet her brother. That time in my life is so foggy. I was so high all the time. I swear I haven't touched anything since I found out I was pregnant with Marleigh. I haven't even had a cigarette, which I stopped cold turkey. I am set on being the best mommy I can be for her. Too much is at risk."

Angel turned back to the window after placing a blanket across Marleigh's back. She knew she shouldn't hold her like this all the time. She will never make any apologies for wanting to have her this close all the time.

"You know her portable cradle is literally right here next to Maia," Marlow joked. "No pressure though. In the middle of the night when you're trying to sleep, she's going to want you to pick her up and hold her."

Angel giggled and kissed Marleigh's fat cheek.

"I know and I will get up and pick her up. Thanks to you and Joey, I can do that without thinking about our next meal or whether we will have a place to live with a roof over our heads. Thank you for everything you're doing for us. You and Joey have a wonderful life here. I'm glad I can be a part of it."

Angel again turned to the window and looked up and then down the street.

"You know, checking for him every five seconds won't make him arrive any sooner."

Angel exhaled and turned to her as if she were puzzled.

"What? Who?" she questioned innocently.

"Girl, don't go there with me. You're checking for Horace. He'll be here soon. He's finishing up your bathroom and putting the new doors on, the main door and the glass storm door. That green you picked out is going to be beautiful."

"It's a close match to the front door on the main level. I think he's adding a separate alarm system for that level today too. He mentioned that last night," Angel noted.

"Oh? Do tell. I was tired of keeping y'all company. How late did he stay?"

Angel opened her mouth to answer and then stopped. She knew what her sister was setting her up for.

"Don't try it. I know what you're doing."

"Me? I'm doing something?"

Marlow walked over to her and looked out of the window just as she had done; looking up and then down the street. When Horace showed up, he usually parked on the corner across the street from the house with his truck or his car facing the house.

"I'm not looking for Horace. I'm just looking at all of the people walking back and forth. It's a beautiful day. Delores isn't coming by today, is she?" Angel asked.

She was still getting used to their mother again. It was taking some getting used to her overbearing, no thought to what she says, kind of interaction.

"Oh, god, no. She's a lot and I'm not in the mood. I haven't heard from her. Have you?"

"It's been quiet."

"True. Wait until she finds out you have the hots for Horace's fine ass. Don't try and deny it. It's me. I know you."

"What? I do not."

Angel tried to deny the obvious. It may work with someone else, but not with her sister.

"You do and he has the hots for you too."

"It's too soon. I should focus on Marleigh and not a man."

"You can't multi-task? First of all, Horace isn't just any man. He's a good man. I can't speak for all the men you've connected with, which is a good way to say, hooked up with or been involved with, but Horace is on a different level all together. There is no timing on being interested in a good man. You can be her mother while also getting to know him. I would rather you do that, and do it now while you're here and I can help with Marleigh. Not that I will ever rush you to move out because Joey already made it clear that you can stay here with us forever and I agree. I'm just saying, if you like him, there is no harm in that. I see how he looks at you. It's the same way you look at him. There is nothing wrong with it. Girl, that man not only helped you feed your daughter who was getting fussy when her peaches were running out and you had to stop feeding her to get more, but he cleared the table and loaded the dishwasher. This is a man who could hire a whole team of people to cook his food, clean up and wash the dishes. Y'all were so cute. I had to get out of the way. That's when I exited stage left. He wasn't here for us; he was here for you. If you're looking out of that window in anticipation of him showing up, I love it. He's a giant leap up from Santiago, for sure."

Angel closed her eyes and pictured him before a cold chill caused her to shake off any thoughts of him. To hear what he'd done to Marlow, she could wring his neck.

"I can't believe he kidnapped you and had plans to kill you. How could he blame you for Angelo's death? I'm glad he's in prison. He won't be able to hurt you again; or me, for that matter."

When Marlow didn't answer, but placed a hand on her shoulder, she waited. They'd had a few heavy conversations over the past week about Santiago. She had revealed many secrets to Marlow.

"Are you ever going to tell me why you didn't confide in me that he was hitting you? He blamed me and Steven for your drug use when it was him who helped keep you high around the clock all so that he could keep you under his thumb. I wish you had talked to me. I wasn't being a good big sister if you didn't feel you could come to me for help. I don't think he ever really wanted me to stay with you in Florida. He talked a good game, though. I get it. I'm just sorry you went through all of that. Yes, Steven was wrong for introducing you to drugs as a teenager. Santiago played on that. All I can say is, you're now free. You're free to make a life for you and Marleigh and do whatever you want to do. The sky is the limit and I'm going to help you. For now, continue to strengthen your bond with Marleigh. You have some time before you have to either go to school or get a job according to the court. You have a counseling session next week, right?"

"I do. I'm looking forward to unpacking a lot that's been holding me down. I'm ready for all things new and better."

Angel gazed out of the window again and this time, an excitement raced through her body causing her to rock back and forth to try and contain her joy. Horace's large, white Chevrolet Silverado pulled up to the corner, turned slightly to the right before backing up to his usual spot. She smiled at the thought that he had a usual spot in front of their house.

"Uh, oh. Your knight in shining truck must have arrived. You're acting all brand-new and stuff!"

"Very funny, sis. That man is so fine, isn't he? I mean, he's really handsome but so much more than that. Do you think he likes me? I know you said it, but do you really believe that? Perhaps, he's just being nice."

"I know it to be true. Just go with it. Trust me when I say, you and Horace have my blessing if you pursue anything. He was the first to jump in with help after you called to tell me you were in trouble. He's been here since day one. He showed up to support your first appearance in family court when he didn't have to. After all, he's in the middle of building a casino with a fourteen-story hotel above it. The man is busy, but he was there. He offered to help with the updates we need to have done to the downstairs apartment. He got right on that. The man is handy, that's for sure. He's been looking in on both of us since Joey has been out of town. Not that he isn't doing it to help me, but he's really doing it for you and Marleigh. You see how he loves this little one. She loves him too. She gets excited like you do when she sees him. He hits her with that pearly white, toothy grin and her little arms don't stop reaching out for him until he picks her up. Her little pats on his cheeks are adorable. He's not here out of obligation. He's

73

here because he wants to help you and most of all, because he likes you. A man who really wants to show you who he is and who he can be for you will do the things that he's doing. Most will focus on trying to get to the next level without fulfilling what needs to be at level one. Horace is a class act."

Angel bit her lower lip and held on to it with her teeth. She was hopeful that what Marlow was saying was true.

"I hope so. I like him, Mar. I'm hesitant because of my history with men, but he is definitely different; in a good way."

"That he is. Listen, I'm going to take both girls with me upstairs. Hand me Marleigh. It's time to put her down anyway. I have some online consultations I need to get to. I'll put them in their cribs. I'll let you know when she's up. You need to go down and let Horace and his men in. I see a big truck pulling up in front of the door. That's them."

Angel handed Marleigh over. She fussed for a second after her sleep was disturbed, but she fell right back to sleep. Marlow picked up Maia in her other arm and moved slowly up the steps with them.

"I love you, Mar. You are a great big sister. Never doubt that."

Marlow winked and blew a kiss to her, being careful not to speak too loud as to not wake up either baby.

Angel started to get up from her seat at the window when she stopped after noticing that Horace hadn't gotten out of his truck. From what she could see, he was in a deep conversation with someone on his cell phone. Whoever it was, they had his undivided attention. He was focused on that person and what they were saying. She shuttered at the thought that maybe, unbeknownst to her and Marlow, Horace may have a woman in his life. That thought saddened her. She was really hoping beyond all hope that he was single and as interested in her as she was in him. Shaking it off, she still got up and headed toward the lower level. When his call ended, he would still need to get inside of the house. She hoped his call wasn't anything bad. He wasn't smiling and seemed quite serious. Perhaps it was a woman and they were having a disagreement. She stopped letting her mind take her anywhere other than what was the reality. She merely had to wait and see. She was a new person. She was ready to take life one day at a time.

7

"Asia, can you let me get a word in, please?" Horace pleaded.

"*Asia?* Since when do you call me Asia? You always call me Ace like everyone else."

Horace leaned his head in his hand, speaking loudly in his truck through the dashboard system. He and Ace had been on the phone ever since he left the casino. The conversation wasn't a good one.

"I'm just saying that you're reading more into this than there actually is. You and I were never exclusive. We never even mentioned the word relationship. All of a sudden, you're talking about a future together and taking things to the next level. I don't get what that level is because as far as I knew, we were never on any level. We were having fun."

"Fun, Horace? Yes, we were having fun, but that's all this was to you? Yes, we have had the wildest sex of my entire life. I've never had a man give me multiple orgasms back-to-back. We are amazing together in the bedroom. I was thinking we should consider more. I wanted to talk about that before you return to Vegas after the casino opening. It's been months. I've been starving for you. Don't you miss all of this? Do you want to guess what I'm doing right now?"

He could only imagine. Right now, he didn't even want to do that. His eyes were focused on Angel who was sitting in the window looking right at him. At first, she was all smiles.

Suddenly, her smile disappeared. He'd been thinking about her all day. Being anxious to see her today was an understatement. His excitement was on cloud-nine and then Ace called him. He started not to answer but decided it was time they had a talk about how aggressive she was suddenly being about what they were to each other. He'd always seen them as sex buddies. Something about that had changed for her ever since he'd been in Chicago. He was trying to understand what had happened.

"You are not speaking as the same woman that you have been since I met you. Since when do you want to be exclusive with anyone, namely, me? This is new and I'm a little or actually, a lot confused. I'm not looking for a relationship. I'm definitely not looking for something long distance which is what this would have to be."

"What? Why is that? You're not coming back to Vegas?"

After his talk with Torrence and now after meeting Angel, he'd made his decision. He was ready for a life right here in Chicago. He was planning to stay. On his walk to his truck at the casino, he was already thinking about reaching out to a realtor to find him a nice townhouse or condo that he could buy. He didn't want to live at the casino hotel permanently. It was nice to have the space on those long days and nights when after work, all he wanted to do as get some quick sleep. He was now thinking of a more long-term relocation.

"I've decided that I'm not going to return to Vegas other than to pack up my place and ship everything here. I'm going to be house hunting soon and I don't plan on buying a bunch of new stuff since my suite at the casino was fully furnished by me."

"You're not coming back? What the hell, Horace? When were you going to say something? You've left me hanging all these months on the promise that you wanted to see me. You even asked me to come to Chicago to see you. What was that all about? Sex? It was about sex? That's something you can get from any woman, like I know you were doing anyway. Men like you and Torrence don't settle, though I'm still wondering what that woman he married has between her legs that snagged him. I hear he now has a baby besides getting married. That's something because he was slinging that thing all over Las Vegas, just like you. What? Did you find a few new women to slide up in while in Chicago? I'm not just some play thing, Horace. I have feelings, you know."

"Whoa, wait a minute. We've had one conversation about us and that was when we first started messing around. I told you then that I wasn't interested in anything serious with any woman. You were good with that. If I'm correct, that conversation actually took place after we had wild sex on that first night that we met. We agreed on a physical thing only. I thought you were down for that to the point that when it was over, it would just be over."

"Oh, so, you screw my brains out quite a few times each week and you think that was all I was ever going to be to you? I thought you'd come around. I'm Asia Wingate. Did you hear me? I can have any man I want. I am gorgeous, vivacious and bodacious! Men throw themselves at me every day. You're going to miss out on me if you don't take us seriously. I may like moving to Chicago if that's what we would work out. We never talked about anything. Anytime we're together, some part of your body had my mouth occupied."

Horace laughed to himself at the image she just put in his head. The one thing Ace was not, was shy.

"Okay, let's pull it back. Listen, I have something I need to get to. I'm in my truck and I reached my destination. I'm sorry if you felt misled, though I don't see how. I think we should both just move on. I'm sure you are not short on men burning up the sheets with you. Let's do this conversation another time, if there is more to be said. I need to go."

"Wait, Horace. Can I still get tickets to the grand opening of the casino? You did promise me and my friends an invite along with a few rooms comped for a few days following that. Maybe we can talk again about that. I know you're a busy man. Take some time and think about it. Think about what we could be as a power couple. You a casino owner and me one of the biggest poker players in the world. After all, I am *Ace of Spades* and no one can turn me down. I run the entire deck called life, baby."

"I will still get your invite to you and yes, your rooms will be comped. We can talk then but I'm not going to compromise on what we agreed we would be."

"Maybe even hit me off with all that power between your legs while I'm there, for old time's sake. Why can't we be at the start of something new?"

"Ace?"

"Okay, okay, I hear you. Do what you need to do. Call me, okay? I think we need to talk more about this. You're not seeing the full picture of us. Even my name is in your name. You're Horace and I'm Ace. We're like peanut butter and jelly; like bacon and eggs, like Jim and Chrissy."

"Who?"

"You know."

"I don't think I do."

"Jim Jones and Chrissy Lampkin. She's my idol. I love her!" Ace kidded.

Horace had to laugh. He remembered a few conversations about the couple.

"You are crazy, Ace. I'll give you a call."

"You better. Keep it long, thick and hard for me. Hopefully, one day, just for me?"

"Later, Ace."

When the call ended, Horace looked back up to the window and was sad when he didn't see Angel's beautiful smile looking back at him.

When the men in the truck finally stepped out in front of Marlow's house, he hopped out of his truck after grabbing his phone from the cradle and raced over. As soon as he got there, the door to the lower level opened and there stood a magnificent sight. He would never, ever tire of being greeted by her and hoped that after he finished his work, he would still be welcomed over to see her and Marleigh. He was counting on it because even though he readily admitted that what he and Ace had was over, he was planning on a new beginning that he'd never planned for. He was going to ask Angel out on a date. What happens after that would be up to her. He was keeping hope alive that she was open to at least a dinner date.

"Hi beautiful," he said walking down the few steps to the lower level.

"Hi yourself. It's good to see you again, Horace."

He loved the way she spoke his name. He would love to hear it a million times more.

"It's lovely to be seen again. Can we bring everything in?"

"Yes. Mi casa es su casa," she responded.

Horace leaned closer to her so that his men couldn't hear. "I'll hold you to that one day."

8

One week later and Angel stood at the closed door to the lower level of the house where Horace informed them the night before that the updates were completed. All of the furniture was in place and she and Marleigh could finally move into what would now be their new apartment. She had to make a promise to Horace and Marlow that she wouldn't go downstairs to take a look until they were all together. Horace was adamant that he wanted to be there when she took her first look at the final setup. To make sure she wasn't tempted, he had gone as far as putting a large ribbon on the door to make sure he and Marlow would be able to tell if she snuck down anyway.

Marleigh was awake and so was Maia. She had Marleigh in her arms. She was fascinated at her little self that she had learned how to spit bubbles, a habit they weren't sure where she picked that up from. Marlow held Maia and Horace was taking his time taking the ribbon off.

"Could you go any slower? Dinner will burn in the oven by the time you get that ribbon off. Come on!" Angel declared playfully while Horace began moving in slow motion to drag out the excitement even more.

"I'll still eat it even if it's burned. It's not too often I get invited for a home cooked meal," he said.

"Lies. All lies. Marlow and I invite you to have dinner with us almost every time you're here working on the house. We feed you well over here. Besides, there is no doubt you worked up an appetite on the fix ups. Before you told me I could no longer go down until the last piece of furniture was in place, I could see the hard work you put in. Now, all I want to do is go down those steps to my new apartment."

"What's for dinner?" Horace asked, winking at both Angel and Marlow.

They knew he was making them sweat. Marleigh, on the other hand kept reaching for him to hold her. Angel finally gave in and handed her over.

"I swear my own child is a traitor. How can she prefer you over me?" she questioned jokingly.

"She knows a good-looking man when she sees one. She's a typical female," Marlow laughed.

"Okay ladies. Here we are at this momentous occasion. I feel like a speech is in order," Horace started before Angel tapped him playfully on the arm.

"If you weren't holding my baby, I would push you down those stairs. Move out of the way. You can save that speech for dinner. I want to see. Come on!" she jibed.

"Okay, okay. Go ahead. I'll bring up the rear with my favorite girl in my arms."

Before he could get out another word, Angel moved around him and went down first. Marlow followed right behind her. When she looked back, Horace was talking baby talk to Marleigh as they brought up the rear. To say she was shocked at the difference in the space didn't describe what she was seeing. The idea that she and Marleigh were going to have their own space invigorated her.

"Wow! Just wow. This is so nice. Marleigh is going to love it here just as much as I know I will, at least until you and Joey make a decision about whether you're going to move or not," Angel said.

Once they were all in the apartment and looking around, Horace walked up and tried to hand Marleigh back to her. To all of their amazement, her daughter didn't want anyone but Horace.

"Your sister and Joey are moving?" he asked her when Marlow went to check out the bedrooms.

Angel decided to go see the kitchen area to see the new backsplash in aqua and white, the main color scheme of her kitchen.

"This is just amazing. I mean, I love it all. You didn't let me see what the backsplash would look like before you put it up. You said I would love it and I do. And Marlow said they were thinking about moving to a place with more privacy. Joey is so well known that he feels off of his game when he's out of town and worrying about their safety. He wants a property that has more privacy from the public being able to walk right up to the door. I get that. He told me that if they did decide to move that Marleigh and I would always have a home with them if that's what I want. For now, this is best for me. I don't think I'm ready for a place with just my daughter and I. Having all of this support close by is what will help me get to where I need to be."

"I agree on them moving. I see people driving my and scoping out where Joey Dreads lives, all the time when I'm here. Until Marlow and Maia are traveling with him, he will always worry. Then that means they would worry about you and Marleigh being here alone. I would worry too."

"I wouldn't want anyone to worry about us. I love the living room furniture. Marlow, you picked the perfect sectional for me. This is all so overwhelming," Angel explained.

"It's all yours, sis. For as long as you want to stay with us, we will always have a place for you and my niece."

"I need to show you how the new alarm system works. I had a guy out to finish the installation yesterday while you were at your counseling session. How did it go, if I can ask without prying?" Horace questioned.

"Oh, you're not prying. It went well. I didn't realize how much stuff in me I really needed to speak on and release. I'm going to like this counselor. She isn't one that was recommended by the judge. Joey met with a counselor after the car accident put him on his behind for a while. I didn't use his counselor but one who works in the same office. We're meeting weekly for now. I was sad I missed seeing you yesterday. I'm getting used to you being around. Clearly, Marleigh feels the same way. She won't even come to me when you're here. She loves you."

"I am in love with her just as much. She brings so much light to my day. When I didn't get a chance to see her yesterday because you all were gone all day, I felt slighted like I had really missed out on something important. Besides, she and I have long, healthy talks about her day. I hear you switched out her strawberries for bananas and she wasn't happy about it," he laughed.

"She tells all of our secrets, doesn't she," Angel added.

"You know what – I missed you too. Seeing you is the best part of any day. I wanted you to know," Horace leaned over and whispered close to her ear.

He gave her the floor to go in any direction she wanted. Now was her chance.

"I missed you too. I do believe I smile more when you're around. Will you still come around now that the work is done or are you done having us interrupt the work you need to focus on at the casino?"

"Well, I am a phone call away. You can call me at any time, day or night and I'll be here. Even if it's just to keep you company or to talk. I'm here for you."

Angel touched his arm lightly. In the next breath, they laughed when they noticed Marleigh looking to where her hand was on Horace as if she was saying that she didn't like anyone touching him but her. She quickly moved her hand away.

"Okay, I get it, baby girl. When he's here, you don't want to share. I can understand that."

Angel followed Horace to the front door so that he could go over how the alarm works. He also showed her how to change the passcode to something only she and Marlow would know. They then ventured to check out the full bathroom, Marleigh's newly decorated room and of course, the master bedroom with the walk-in-closet that Horace's team built for her. Lastly, they checked out the master bathroom. She was surprised to see that he'd also added a powder room on the outside wall of the bathroom. She liked that. This way, she didn't have to let guests use her private bathroom.

"Love it?" Marlow asked. "Is this enough space for you and my niece?" she added.

"Are you kidding me? This is perfect. I couldn't ask for anything better than this. I can come and go and not disturb you and Joey. I can't wait to cook in my own kitchen."

"Maybe you can make something and invite Horace over for dinner so that I don't have to be a third wheel until my hubby gets home. He'll be back next week. He facetimes with me and Maia every day, but that's nothing compared to him being here. I'm going up to check on dinner. The two of you can continue to check things out. You did great Horace. I appreciate you, considering, I know what your life is like. The way you jumped in and coordinated all of this in Joey's absence is a blessing," Marlow said.

"I would do it again a million times even if he was here. I would do anything for all of you, especially these two. Do you want to see the new room you didn't know was on the other side of the kitchen?" Horace asked.

"What room? There's a room back there? I thought it was laundry."

"Well, there is a small laundry room back there. You won't have to go all the way up to the top floor to do that. There is also an office with a desk and other office stuff that Marlow ordered. I think she's waiting on a computer to come for you. She mentioned you were thinking of going to school part-time even though you're also looking for work. All I did was separate the kitchen from that room with a wall and voila, another space. This house, for a brownstone, is huge."

"Ah!" Angel shrieked and then ran to the back of the apartment and into her very own office. She looked and Horace and Marleigh weren't with her. She took the time to look around the space to think of the possibilities. She knew that she would do everything in her power to not let anyone down, especially herself.

She turned and went back out into the family room to find Horace playing with Marleigh as she held and twisted a gray stuffed elephant that was in the portable crib next to the sectional. With the large screen television on the wall in front of the sofa, she already knew that this would be her favorite spot.

"You like?" he asked, looking up at her from his place on the newly carpeted floor in hues of blue to match the décor.

"I love. You and my sister thought of everything."

"Did I forget to tell you that your brother was here with me yesterday? He put the shelves up in the office and in Marleigh's room."

Without warning, Angel began to cry. She tried to hold back her feelings but one thing she learned in counseling was to never do that. Holding true feelings in could be unhealthy. Horace jumped up and pulled her close. She went into his waiting arms. They kept their eye on Marleigh who was on her belly still giving that elephant grief. She was cute and rough, just like her mother.

"Don't cry. What's wrong?"

He held her close.

Angel inhaled his natural scent along with a hint of sexy, smoky musk.

"Everyone has gone above and beyond to help me get a fresh start, including you. I can't thank you enough. I wouldn't even know where to begin."

Horace smiled at her and wiped the few tears that had fallen down her cheeks. He then lifted her head so that their eyes were focused on each other.

"I have two ideas, though you don't owe me anything. How about you invite me over for dinner? I don't want you cooking for me yet. We can either make something together or I can bring something over for us to enjoy together."

She smiled, loving the sound of that.

"What is the other idea? You said you had two or were those two different ideas?"

"The other one is, would you like to go out on a date with me, perhaps to a nice restaurant and maybe some dancing? I'm thinking anyplace other than the casino. I don't want to be too forward, but I also don't want to beat around the bush when it comes to the fact that I like you. I'm not just talking a little bit. I really like you, Angel. I hope my sharing that isn't too soon considering all that's on your plate these days. I don't want to interfere with any of your plans to straighten your life out, as you say. I'm hoping I can be a part of it. What do you think about that?"

Angel trembled at the idea that they were on the same page. She didn't have to wonder anymore if the time they had been spending together was just him doing what he'd promised in looking after them. He had people checking in on them, but Horace was there for her. She liked him too.

"I think I'd like to do both of your ideas. I love cooking, so cooking together would be great. I'd also love to go out with you. We would have to plan that around Marlow so that she can keep the baby when we go out. I like you too, Horace. I have from the moment I looked behind me at the courthouse and you were there with everyone else. The difference was, you were smiling at me. I looked at you and saw that you really cared about what I was going through. Since then, it's been a bonus every time I see you. Thanks for being you."

"Dinner is ready if the two of you are interested. I also put a bottle in the warmer for Marleigh. Come on up or I'm about to eat enough for all three of us. Besides, the food will get cold," Marlow yelled down the stairs at them.

"I guess that's our one-minute warning," Angel joked as Horace picked Marleigh up into his arms.

When she moved toward the steps, Horace reached for her hand and drew her attention back to him.

"One more thing," he said.

When questionable eyes, Angel waited. He didn't make her wait too long.

As his head lowered toward hers, she knew he was waiting for her permission to go further. She nodded her head to let him know that she wanted this as much as he did. And then it happened.

Horace raised his hand to her chin once again. This time, he raised her head slightly and kissed her sweetly on the lips. The kiss didn't last long but it was the most erotic things she's ever experienced. She was used to hurried and rushed kisses. This was sexy. Horace leaned back for a second and then moved in for another kiss. This one was thorough and methodical. His skill was unmatched to any other time in her life when she'd been kissed. His hand went behind her long hair so that could meld his lips to hers while holding her close to him. She was all set to kiss for the sake of it, without feeling or thought, the way she'd always kissed. Horace had other plans. He took his time getting acquainted with her lips. He kissed one corner of her lips and then the other before covering her full mouth with his.

The softness of his touch on her lips and the way he held her head had her mind screaming for a whole lot more. He had her feeling so sexy and desired that she would have leaped into his arms if Marleigh wasn't already there with her head on his shoulder. The kiss lasted a minute more before Horace slowly pulled away and let go of her head.

"I've been dying to do that for a long time. This moment seemed like the perfect time. Are you okay?"

Was she okay? Her body, mind and spirit were screaming yes! She was much more than okay. They kissed. She'd been thinking about what it would be like to kiss him. Now she knew and because of that, she wanted more than one kiss.

"I'm perfect," she finally uttered softly.

"Good because now that the first kiss is out of the way, I can't wait to do that again. We'll table that for another time. We had better go save Marlow from overeating!" he quipped.

"Right because if I know my sister, she will do just that."

Angel toward the steps and then stopped again.

"You good?" he asked.

"I am. I just want to say thank you. Thanks for redeeming my idea of men. So many have treated me horribly in such a way that I wasn't sure if I would be interested in anyone again. And then there is you. I didn't know kind, sweet, gentle, caring men like you existed. At the same time, you are all male and you know it. You move with the kind of confidence that I hope to have for myself one day. Thanks for allowing me to not question if I was always going to attract insane men," she acknowledged and smiled.

"Sweetheart, I am who you are experiencing because I'm with you and Marleigh. That's not to say that I'm anything like the guys you've told me you've gone out with. I'm not even close to who they are. Before meeting you, let's just say, I've had interest in women that was of a much faster pace than what I want with you. I'm hoping we can start something that is new to me. I'll tell you more about that after dinner, if you don't mind me hanging around. Luckily, the casino property is closed to everyone until after another inspection tomorrow. I have a free evening, if you feel like sitting and talking later."

"That sounds like a perfect evening to me. I would like that very much."

Angel was glad that she walked up the steps ahead of Horace. She wanted to giggle out loud in the same happy manner that she was feeling. Horace didn't need to see the look of sheer joy and happiness on her face. She even touched her finger to her lips where his had been minutes before. Like him, she was looking forward to another powerful kiss like that one. It's clear she'd been missing out on kissing with passion and not just for the sake of getting naked. She could only imagine what that would be like with him. She put that behind when they reached the kitchen to find Maia in a baby bouncer on the table and Marlow about to say grace without them. Angel looked at her impatiently.

"What? I told y'all to hurry up. I am hungry. Are you staying for dinner and dessert, Horace?"

Angel caught his gaze when he looked to her for confirmation.

"Yes, he is. We're going to relax later on, if that's okay with you. We'll clean up the kitchen, as we usually do and then we're going to watch some television in my new apartment," Angel said. "Is that okay with you?" she asked him.

"Like you said, that sounds like a perfect evening to me."

9

Horace had waited nervously in Angel's apartment while she finished getting ready for their date. If he thought that at any time in his life he couldn't be moved to a vulnerable state, he was dead wrong. The minute she walked out of her bedroom in her little black dress and her long hair pulled up high on her head giving him a birds-eye view of her strikingly elegant neckline, he was a goner. So far, he'd only seen her dressed down in comfortable clothing.

Sitting across the table from her at the restaurant, he'd been unable to focus on anything but the fine woman across from him. The red lipstick on her perfectly formed lips was singing a song of desire on a level that was a magnitude equal to out of this world. Of all the women he's been with over the years, Angel seemed to be the one that had him thinking of more than just sex. He was actually teetering on the precipice of love.

He kept trying to find words to invoke a meaningful conversation but every time he went to open his mouth, all he wanted to do was compliment her on everything he'd come to know about her that he loved. Adding to the yearning his heart was developing since they arrived was the soft music being played by a harpist in the center of the restaurant. The atmosphere was definitely set to one focused on love. There was no doubt that when he asked Torrence about a restaurant that was a favorite of him and Reese, his friend had decided to introduce him to some place along the lines of romance.

"How was your fish?" he finally asked her.

When she looked up from the table with soft eyes and features, Horace had to shake his head to be more in the moment and less on how far into the future his mind was roaming. In it, he saw his future and it included Angel and Marleigh. For the first time in his life, he was thinking about what his life would look like with his own family.

"If there is a word to describe something that would be beyond perfect, that would be the word. I've been missing out. I thought you made the best glazed salmon when we cooked dinner together last week at my place. I have to admit, this was worth getting all dolled up for. Of course, my first reason was for you and then for this dinner," she smiled.

Horace's heart did a happy dance.

"I'm sorry I messed up our plans for a dinner date last week. There was a lot going on at the casino. I've started the hiring process for additional staff. We received hundreds of resumes."

"Are you kidding? I was fine with cancelling the date that night. I see how you run yourself crazy every single day. With Joey being back, I didn't know how often you would still come by."

Horace placed his open hand in the center of the table next to the lighted candle that sat between them. When Angel got the message and placed her hand in his, he cradled it snugly in his.

"There was also a part of me that just wanted to be close to you. With him being back, as you should already be able to tell, I still come around. I don't want to be a pest."

"Oh, never. I would have been ready, like this, that night to go out. More important than going out, I just wanted to see you and spend some time with you. I was ecstatic when you opted instead for us to stay in and cook. I ate that salmon you made for three days in a row. That night was one of the best of my life. I don't ever remember being that relaxed without a care in the world. You're different than the typical type of man I seem to end up with. I attract the worse kind; until you."

"Don't beat yourself up for the choices you've made. Be happy that you have a chance to fix anything that hasn't been working for you."

"Very true. I have a court date coming up in two days. Kris thinks all of the charges will be dropped. Charlie doesn't want what his plan was for me to get out beyond where it has already been. She told me that his wife found out after she was interviewed and he's pissed. I didn't mean to blow up his life. I'm not that kind of person," she humbly said.

"Don't fret. He dug this grave for himself. He's supposed to protect and serve. He wasn't representing the uniform well. Serves him right."

"That's what my sister and Kris said. It seems that she was able to find a few other women he'd done things to; horrible things. I thought about my daughter and was fed up with always putting myself in stupid situations. The woman Marleigh and I were staying with confessed that she lied because he told her to. He gave her money. I was giving her as much as I could money-wise each month. Still, she kept telling me to find ways to get her more for all that she was doing for us. I was between a rock and a hard place."

"But never again, right?"

If it were up to him, she would never be that low again.

"Never, ever. Once this is over this week, I can focus on signing up for on-line classes and hopefully finding a job.

Marlow will watch Marleigh for me while I work. Once I get custody of Marleigh back, she plans to travel more with Joey."

"How's the situation with child services going? Any progress?"

"I'll know next week. There is a scheduled visit at the house. Marlow and I are excited to show them the new apartment. Kris thinks I'll be in a better position to be able to take Marleigh out and about on my own once I have at least a part-time job. Taking classes is something I've wanted to do for a long time."

Their waitress placed their desserts on the table, two slices of chocolate lover's cake in front of them.

"I was thinking of taking this slice to go but now that I see it, that's not going to happen," Horace said just before slicing his fork through the delicious moist cake.

When Angel moaned on the other side of the table, the world stopped moving for him. His fork stopped midway to his mouth. He honed in on her expression in response to the piece of cake that she'd just placed in her mouth. When her tongue licked across her lips, he was done for. All the kissing they'd been engaging in came to mind. He would give his right arm to kiss her right now. Her sweetness along with the sweet cake would be his world's delight. He smiled when she caught him staring at her mouth. He wasn't shy about his desire for her. For once in his life, he was able to keep it in check until the time was right for both of them.

"Are you okay? You suddenly stopped moving like a glitch in a movie."

Her words shook him back to life. He put his fork down.

"I'm sorry about that. You are just so damn beautiful. Everything about you is incredible. I don't want you to think I'm only speaking of your outward beauty. I'm being honest when I say you make me want to be better so that I can be more to you. I guess I want to prove myself to you. I want to be worthy beyond what other men have brought into your life."

"Horace, you don't have to prove anything special to me. I'm the one who is trying to figure out how a man like you, who could have any woman you want, has an interest in me. I've been nothing but trouble; hurting my own life and future. Surely, you have been interested in women of a greater caliber than me. You own casinos. You're rich, fine as hell and have so much more going for you. I would barely survive if it wasn't for my sister. I would still be struggling just to make ends me. In truth, I still am until I find a job. I want to be my own woman. I want to be sure that when my daughter looks up at me, I am someone she would be proud of. I'm not there yet, but I'm going to devote my entire life to getting there. Are you sure I am who you're interested in?"

He had an idea that he wanted to kick himself for not thinking of it before.

"I'm more than sure. In fact, I may have another way to help you. I want you to succeed in everything you do. If I can help in any way, I will do that. I hope you don't see it as charity. I care about you. I care about Marleigh. You're not a case for me or someone I need to fix. I know that's been going through your mind because of the conversations we've had. I'm not trying to make up for my past by helping you in my present. I want to date you and show you that I'm worthy of your time and energy. I want to admit something to you."

"Okay."

"I don't date. I mean, I've never actually dated. I have had female friends that were more like friends-with-benefits. Being with women has always been about the physical for me since I was a teenager. That's when I got my first taste of sex. I'm being totally transparent when I say that the minute I met you, my take on relationships with women has changed. I want to focus on being that man for you and you being that woman for me; no others. I want to give a relationship a try and I want to do that with you."

"What about when you leave to go back home?"

"I've decided I'm not doing that. I love the life I've been making for myself here. Sin city is fun, but it's not a life for me anymore. I have friends here who are more like family. There is also you and Marleigh. I'm drawn to seeing if anything can grow between us if you're open to that. We're at your pace, and yours only. I don't want to be another man who takes advantage of any part of you. Being in something with you, together, is my goal. What about you?"

Angel put her fork down and pushed the cake to the side. He waited as she gathered her thoughts.

"I must be dreaming. Can this really be my life? Can I really have someone like you in my life after all I've been through? It seems unreal, just like this night. When I knew this date was happening, Marlow got my hair and nails done. She also took me shopping for this dress. I don't know that I've ever had a makeup artist beat this face like this before, but I loved it. Getting pretty for you felt good. I wanted to do it for you but mostly for me. I love feeling pretty. I love the way you look at me and how being with you makes me feel. When I came out of the bedroom and you saw me, my legs were weak. I've had men look at me with lust in their eyes before. With you, I see your desire for me, but there is also so much more. Your interest in me radiates from your heart. I feel that. I would be out of my mind to not want you in my life. Marleigh loves you more than me, that's obvious."

They laughed together.

"That means she's already on my side if it comes to a vote. It would be me and her for the win!" he declared loudly.

When others around them gazed his way because of his outburst, Angel had to cover her own mouth because she was laughing so hard.

"I would deny all of that, but you're right. I say yes to you and to us. I don't know where it will go. I'm happy to be moving forward with you."

Horace stood in the midst of the best talk he's ever had. He went around to her side of the table and leaned down when she turned her head to face him.

"I hope these folks didn't mind my loudness. If so, they'll hate this. I'll apologize after," he said. "This red lipstick has my name written all over it. I need just a little taste," he added.

Before Angel could react, he moved forward placing his lips against hers passionately, drawing her breath into his mouth as he kissed her with all that he had in him. Angel's hands went to either side of his face, caressing his cheeks as he deepened the kiss the moment she moaned when their tongues found each other. His one hand circled the column of her neck as her lips hungrily took what she needed from the ardent encounter. Her lips were sweeter than he'd been imagining all night. Devouring her mouth when they were alone was always on his agenda. Doing so publicly like this was as natural as breathing. With Angel, everything felt right.

This, he knew wasn't anything temporary. With Angel, they are creating a future.

When patrons at other tables around them began to clap, Horace stood to his full height, looked around and waved to them before taking his seat.

"I guess they enjoyed the show. I know I loved being the recipient," Angel said.

After he sat down, he took her hand again and this time he kissed her open palm and the back of her hand. He saw the red from her lipstick on her hand and kissed it again before using his napkin to clean his lips.

"I'm happy to oblige. Oh, before I forget because kissing you fogs my mind, I want you to consider something. I know you're looking for a job. I may have one for you. I brought over the main office executive assistant from the Vegas office to Chicago to oversee the interviews and training of the casino office staff. We have some people in place but we, of course, need a lot more. The casino is operating around the clock. We want our executive office opened and operating around the clock as well. Would you like to interview for one of the office positions?"

"Me? I don't have any skills in that area. I want to take up communications when I sign up for my college courses, but I don't have any background. What would I need to know?"

"I could easily hire you and no one would say a word. Eventually, they will all know that we're seeing each other. I don't want to keep that a secret to have it become some kind of office fodder. I also don't care about that. I think with your bubbly, friendly, kind and caring personality, you would be good as one of the three main receptionists who greet and take care of anyone who is coming in for a meeting with me or the leadership team. You don't need any skills for the job, so don't worry about that. You will be trained on everything from answering the phones, to scheduling travel and meetings.

Triaging whatever needs to be handled is a big part of the job. There is a lot to do in that position and I think you would be perfect for it. I want to help you. I also don't want to just put you there. I want you to feel comfortable about the position. Doing this would also satisfy the court when it comes to you being able to take care of Marleigh on your own if you choose. It pays very well – with everyone with the same type of position making the same salary. There is always room for growth, which you would get on your own with no meddling from me."

"You're serious, aren't you? Do you believe I could do the job?"

"With training, absolutely. You can also plan your own schedule. Torrence and I have always allowed our executive team members to work out their own schedules based on their home life. That balance is important. That way if someone needs to work at night, during the day, overnight – we accommodate that. With you taking care of Marleigh and also planning on taking classes, you can work with, Rhonda, who will be your boss, and plan out a schedule that works for you. Everyone gets a sign-on bonus that goes a long way toward preparing for the opening of the casino. Some people are moving here from other states and cities. We make it easy for them to do so."

"What about my legal situation?" she asked.

"The only place that would matter is on the casino floor in any of those jobs. All you need is a willingness to learn and the friendly disposition that you already have. Think about it. You don't have to decide tonight. I want you to know that the option is there. If you're interested, I'll have Rhonda schedule you for a chat with her and she'll give you more details. Training would start in about two weeks. Our executive staff are all starting the month before the opening. Everything you need to know, you will learn. There will also be others there to help you because we only hire staff who don't see each other as competition, but see that the focus is on the success of the casino and hotel, not just them individually. Again, think about it. Until then, let's decide about how we're going to celebrate when Kris gets your case dropped in a few days. I'm already declaring it because there is no way that you've come this far for anything to hold you back like that case. How does all of that sound?"

"It sounds like you are the most wonderful man I've ever met. It feels good to be me. It feels even better to be on this side of your affection. I want to say thank you, but you keep telling me to stop thanking you for being you. Still, I want you to know that it all matters to me; you matter to me. That kiss matters to me so much that I'm ready to take this dessert home with me to enjoy it. Perhaps, if the rest of your evening is free, we can finish watching that movie we started the other night before you had to leave. I'm especially interested in more kissing," she offered with a wink and a kiss sent his way.

"More kissing indeed."

10

Marlow raced to grab her cellphone after it rang for the third time. Her focus had been on getting Marleigh and Maia down for a nap. She had three phone consultations coming up with clients over the next two hours. Hopefully both girls would take a long nap after she played with them all morning to tire them out after breakfast. When Joey's handsome face appeared on her screen, she answered quickly.

"Hi, baby!" she hollered.

She then shushed herself before looking into the portable crib in the family room to make sure her greeting hadn't woken either of them up.

"Did you just shush yourself?"

"The girls just went down for an afternoon nap. I was going to go upstairs and do laundry while they slept but they are peaceful. I don't want to rock the boat. I almost lost my sanity when the phone rang. I thought I had it in my back pocket on vibrate. It was on the dining room table. I miss you. How are things going?"

Joey and his brother had taken a flight out the night before to meet with their New York security crew. With them having offices in several cities around the country, they liked to check in with them in-person when time permitted. It was seldom they went together so that they could cover more ground. This time was different. The New York office was moving into a new office suite.

"Great. Carlos got up early to oversee the move into the new digs. I have to say it's a nice building. It's new construction. After this trip, I'll be home for a few months. I think like five or six. I need a break. After the wrestling match at the new casino, that's it for me for a minute. I'm not scheduling anything that doesn't involve my girls. How's Maia? I miss her chubby little cheeks and those thunder legs."

"She's good. She misses her daddy just like I do. It's been nice having you home for the past few weeks. Now you're talking about months with us. I love the idea of that."

"Good because we need to plan some time away. With the criminal charges being dropped against Angel, she can get her fresh start and put that behind her. It will also go a long way to her getting custody of Marleigh back. How are they doing?"

Marlow agreed. Things have been going so well with Angel living with them. Her sister was finally making good strides in life and it appears, in love as well. Being proud and happy for her sister was an understatement.

"Wonderful. I have Marleigh to myself today, which I'm happy about. Angel is getting used to her apartment. She and Marleigh go down there and are making that place a home more and more every day. We try to feed the girls together and let them have playtime together. She's at her job interview today. Remember, I told you about that before you left for your flight."

"Right, the one Horace set up for her at the casino. Was she excited?"

"She was more than excited. She spent yesterday researching what others in the receptionist arena do and how they do it. She refused to let me buy her a new outfit for the interview. Instead, she opted for raiding my closet. If she gets the job, she'll get a sign-on bonus that will cover her first two weeks. She said she wants to be able to take care of herself. The home visit was great with child services. They loved the apartment and Marleigh's room. They told us that for Angel's next family court date, they look forward to giving a glowing update in Angel's favor. Marleigh is getting so big. And she's a very happy baby who loves her mommy. Angel is thriving in that lane."

"Babe, she's remembering Angelo. She wants to make sure that she's not making any of her old mistakes. She's lucky to have a big sister like you who cares about her and the path she's on. Do you have any concerns or reservations about what's growing between her and Horace? It's been a few weeks. Last week, they seem to be getting pretty close."

Marlow nodded as if Joey could see her. She'll facetime with him later.

"He's good for her. She's driven like I've never seen her before. I was concerned early on about her slipping back into her old ways, but she's not interested in looking back. I told her that there is nothing in her past for her anymore. She's also signing up for online classes for the next semester at community college. She did her own research and found that she could attend for free. Things are looking up for her. I'm just happy that she reached out and allowed us to help her along the way. Horace being interested in her is a bonus."

"Do you have any issues with the age difference?" Joey asked.

"None. It's clear that men her age are not on the level that she needs in order to get a good grip on life and her future. He's perfect for her. I think she's in love. I don't know that she ever really was with Santiago. He was more of an escape from a life she hated as a teenager more than anything else. I've never trusted him. I have all trust in Horace. He really likes her. I would say love, but I don't want to be presumptuous. He comes by to see her and Marleigh. He hasn't stayed the night or anything, so I don't think they've gone *there*. I know she's a grown woman, but I do plan to bring up a conversation about condoms later today. After her interview, they're going out to a comedy show at casino West. I think I just talked her up. I hear the door downstairs opening. She does know she can use the door up here if she wants to, right?" Marlow joked.

"I'm sure she does. She's trying her best to make sure we have our privacy as well. I respect that. I'll let you get to your talk with her. I was calling to let you know we landed safe. We were out late last night and I didn't want to ring your phone and wake any of you up. Kiss Maia and Marleigh for me. I'll see you tomorrow night."

"I'll be here waiting with no panties on," she whispered because Angel came through the door and walked up to her.

"I heard that," Angel said, causing them both to laugh. "Y'all are so nasty with it!"

When Angel's attention turned to Marleigh, Marlow walked into the kitchen.

"You know, Angel is keeping both girls tomorrow night, overnight in her apartment so that you and I can have some much-needed quiet time upstairs. I'm thinking hot shower sex, hot hallway sex, hot bed sex, just hot sex all over the place. Oh yeah, somewhere in there, we'll eat dinner. We can also be each other's dessert. I bought something incredibly sexy to wear just for you. It has a little bit of lace and a whole lot of open areas that show all skin and other private areas, all for your pleasure."

"Whew! Don't make me have to take an earlier flight."

"Don't make me dare you."

"Temptress! I love you. Wait until you see what I have for you."

"I'm ready, baby! Hurry home but do it the safe way; by flight!"

"I hear you. I love you."

"I love you too!"

11

"All this *lovey, dovey* stuff! Do you let that man come up for air when he's home?" Angel jibed.

"Only when he needs to breathe! How did the interview go? Is it promising?"

Marlow showed Angel her hands with her fingers crossed for good measure.

"Sis, you will not believe how easy and comfortable that interview was. I went in so nervous. Then I saw all of these other people waiting to be interviewed. They had a look that they had mad skills already. I was a few seconds from turning around and coming back home. For some reason, I felt unworthy. I can be my own worst enemy. The idea of that is why I stayed. I made a promise that I was going to get control of my own life. I held my head up high, crossed these pretty legs and waited my turn. Ms. Rhonda was so gracious. She walked me through a typical day as a receptionist for the executive office. We talked about all of the training I would receive right there onsite. The salary is mad crazy, sis! I mean, mad crazy! I started thinking of all I could do making my own money. I want to give Marleigh the world."

"You mean all the toys and cute little outfits that Horace keeps buying her isn't enough? Now you both will be spoiling her. She still refuses to let go of the elephant her gave her."

Angel put her hands on her hips and then snapped her fingers in the space between them.

"Don't even act like I don't notice all the new clothes in her closet every time I look up. Then there are all of the new books that magically appear. Shall I speak on the cutesy bows, headbands and barrettes for her hair? Who knew a baby her age could have this much hair and it's thick. She already has enough for two long ponytails. It's okay to spoil her. Life could have gone in an entirely different direction for me and her. I want to spoil her every single day. With this new job I have, I will be able to do that while also being able to save some money for the first time in my life."

Marlow looked in Angel's face to be sure she heard what her mind told her she heard. Did she just say?

"You got the job? You got the job!" Marlow screamed before her attempt to lift Angel up off of her feet.

"You can't hold me up and yes, I got the job. My training starts on Monday. I've got five days to prepare. Half of the sign on bonus was given out on the spot once each person signed their contract noting their start date. I need to open up a bank account to deposit my check. I need to have an account for direct deposit going forward. They gave me an employee package that I need to go through. Guess what? I can even sign up for health insurance for me and Marleigh. Good insurance?"

"I'm so proud of you. This all sounds wonderful. What are your hours? Do you know your schedule yet?"

"Well, training is all week from eight to three for the next two weeks. Are you okay with that? I don't want to bog you down. I haven't worked out my actual work schedule yet. I wanted to go over that with you since you will have Marleigh.

Now that I'll be working, I can always find daycare for her. They are offering it at the casino for employees. There is a daycare center opening right next door. Did you know that each of their casinos also own the daycare center on the same property in order to keep those costs down for employees?"

"I didn't know that. It's a great idea and a huge benefit for the employee. No, Angel. She doesn't need a daycare center just yet. She'll be fine right here with me and Maia for the foreseeable future. Joey and I talked about that. After you get custody back, and I'm believing that will be soon, we can revisit the daycare issue. For now, let's not change up her day too much. She loves having her auntie take care of her. She and her cousin have a lot of fun with me entertaining them and reading to them."

"Okay. That's what I thought. What about a work schedule of six in the morning until three in the afternoon? That way, I don't tie up all of your afternoons and evenings."

"That works fine for me. I'm always up early anyway. I'm already working on a routine for both girls. Have you told Horace yet? Does he know? I'm so happy for you!"

"I didn't see him while I was there. I tried to not look around for him. I wanted to stay in professional employee mode. We're going out tonight, remember? I'll call him in a few. I need to eat something. I was so nervous that I didn't eat. I started to see if the rideshare driver could make a quick stop for me to pick up a cheesesteak submarine. Then I thought I would just order us both something good when I got here so that we could celebrate. I wanted to revel in my good news with you first. Good things are happening for me, sis. Can you believe it? Have you ever seen me this happy? Even when I was in Florida, the Sunshine State, I wasn't happy."

"No, and I hope to see it even more. I'm sure that man has a lot to do with all of this happiness you're walking around here with these days. You seem to be getting closer by the day. Anything you want to share?"

"If you're asking me about sex, no we haven't gone there. I know we've been out a few times and he spends a lot of his free time here. We haven't taken that step but I will say that we are officially in a relationship. I've never been happier. He makes my world spin. My entire being is content when I talk to him and when I see him. Are you sure about keeping Marleigh tonight? You've had her all day."

"This time right now is your time. You have no idea how many times I've dream of a time such as this with you. I am so happy and content with my life just like you are with yours. Joey and I have a perfect life together. We move like a well-oiled machine. Nothing gives me more joy than those two girls over there. I love being here with them. I took them out for a walk earlier today and it was the highlight of my morning. I love their little smiling faces. I even love when Marleigh throws a fit because she's got teeth cutting through. She's getting much better at the crawling thing and pulls herself up. You see it and so do I. Little miss independent is a happy baby. That's what matters. We make sacrifices for the people we love. I want everything good for you. Don't fret over the time I spend with them. Focus on enjoying this new life you are crafting for yourself. Love being happy. Love being in love. Don't try to say you're not when I know you are. He's a good man."

Angel started bouncing up and down, clapping her hands.

"He's so *perfect*, isn't he? And he's mine; I'm his. I do love him. I don't want to scare him off by being all clinging and sputtering about love right now. I'm telling you because you're my sister. I know you'll keep my secret. When the time is right, I'll tell him. We're having fun. This is a first for me. There are things around Chicago that I never knew existed when it comes to real, good fun. Horace is showing me all of them. Then he's so loving with me and Marleigh. The other night, I was making her bottles for you to have in case I wasn't here. He was playing with her to keep her busy. When they got quiet, I turned around and both of them were asleep. She was snuggled up right on his chest like it was the most natural thing. Even in sleep, he had a protective, but not too tight hold on her. When she scooted around a bit, he kissed her little cheek and she fell right back to sleep. Horace is everything. Did I tell you that before me, he had not been in a real relationship with a woman? He's been running from something for years. It's kept him from wanting more than something casual; that is, until he met me. We've both been down that path. I want something stable. If he's willing to gamble on me, I'm more than willing to do the same thing."

"I hate to ruin this happy moment, but our mother called. She wants to have a dinner with all of us. I told her it had to be here so that we don't have to transport both girls and all of their stuff. I don't have a date yet, but we'll do it here. If that's too much for you, let me know."

"I'm good with that. I want her to meet Horace so that she can get any negative thoughts about my relationship with him out of the way. I can take it. I'm too happy to let her steal any joy. I also don't want to prolong her response either. It's a good idea. Because I'm in a better place, I'm ready to heal the rift in our family. Marleigh and Maia deserve that. Maybe it will take them to soften Delores up!"

They laughed together. When they want to really get across a point about their mother, they all call her by her first name when the three of them are together.

"From your lips to God's ears! Don't worry about tonight. Besides, you'll have them tomorrow when Joey comes home. We support each other, right? Speaking of supporting you, do you have condoms downstairs?"

Angel doubled over laughing so hard that Marlow waited by tapping her foot nervously on the wood floor feeling like a mother hen.

"Really? You're just going to toss that out like I'm a teenager? I told you we aren't having sex."

"Yet," Marlow said.

"Stop it."

"Oh, but you will. Something tells me that all of this abstaining, yet hot kisses that I'm sure are happening, are about to run their course and lead to the next level. Be prepared. Marleigh does not need a sibling anytime soon. Condoms, Angel. I'm serious. Get some."

Angel huffed, looked all around and then back at her.

"I already have. I picked them up the day after the night Horace asked me about being in a relationship with him while we were out for dinner. I asked him to stop me off at Walmart so that I could pick up some pampers and a few other things for Marleigh. When he went to the electronics area, I had the cashier ring up the condoms before he rejoined me. I bought the kind with a variety of sizes because, well, I don't know that yet, though I suspect only the gold will work. I won't say how I know, but know that I know. I'm prepared. Thanks for looking out. I'm so ready. I feel so close to him. These feelings are not like any I've ever had for anyone else. I know that's easy to say, but it's the truth. I love him, sis. Too soon?" she asked.

"Not if Horace is that person for you. If that's the case, it can never be too soon. Just be careful. At the same time, enjoy the attention of someone like him. As you can see from the company he keeps, these men love for keeps. I discovered that with Joey. Even after I almost killed him when I crashed into his car, once we fell for each other, nothing was ever going to tear us apart. Be ready for that with Horace. He is that type of guy."

"I hear you."

"Good. Now order us some subs with extra meat and tomatoes. Maybe some onion rings too," Marlow said.

Angel went to the drawer in the kitchen where they kept menus.

"You haven't said anything but words. Mar, you know I love you, right? I mean, not just for what you're doing for me now. I've always loved and admired you. I didn't know how to show it or even say it. I'm having the best time here with you and Joey. You've been at the forefront of me making the necessary changes to get ahead. I want you to know that you are an amazing sister; an amazing wife and mother and most of all, an amazing woman."

"You're going to make me cry. You don't have to thank me but I want you to know that I accept it. From your heart to mine and from mine to yours, I love you too."

12

Horace raced around to the passenger side of Torrence's car that was leant to him for the night. He didn't think his truck was sufficient for taking Angel out for the evening. Each time they'd gone out on a date, Torrence was more than happy to let him drive his Porsche. He loved taking Angel out in style. His own preference for rides were definitely any kind of large truck. He'd flown home to Vegas a week after flying into Chicago and drove his truck back with him. His car, a blue Jaguar F-TYPE, was still in Vegas. He was recently thinking that it was time to either have that delivered to him or to pick it up and drive it back to Chicago.

"The comedy show was the best I've ever seen, not that I've seen many others than on television. I saw a show once in Florida when I lived there. I didn't realize JoKoy was that funny," Angel said as they pulled out into traffic after settling into the soft leather.

"He's one of my favorites. We're hoping to get him under contract soon to do a residency here at one of the casinos. He's definitely worth what it will cost. Are you hungry? I know we ate before the show. I didn't want to take you home if you are still starving. That wouldn't be a good move for a boyfriend, huh?" he asked.

When Angel didn't respond, but kept her focus on whatever they were driving past that caught her eye out of the window, he wondered what had suddenly caused her to check out of their conversation.

"No, I guess not," she said solemnly.

Yes, something was wrong. Just that fast, something didn't sit well with her.

"Is something wrong? You've gone quiet on me."

When she didn't respond, he was glad for the red light that they pulled up to.

"Um."

That was all she said.

"Angel, baby, look at me."

He knew that would get her attention. This was the first time he'd called her, baby. The word felt good adding to the atmosphere around them. When he finally saw her eyes, he smiled in hopes that she would smile back. She did just that.

"I'm sorry," she finally said.

"What's wrong?"

With the seat belt restraining most of her movement, she was still able to turn in his direction.

"You're taking me home to my place?"

"Yes. That's what we usually do at the end of a date."

"Are you working early tomorrow?"

"Sort of, yes. Not as early as usual. If you're worried about me getting enough sleep, I promise you I will."

"No, Horace, that's not it. Can I ask you something personal?"

The light changed and he pulled back out into traffic. What he didn't want to do is drive while it seems she really needed to talk about something that was clearly on her mind. Instead, he saw a parking space and pulled over into it.

He removed his seat belt.

"Talk to me. We have always talked about any and everything. You're being mysterious. I'm concerned. What gives?"

"I know I'm not being very upfront. This is all new to me, so bear with me. I like that we go back to the apartment and we hang out and kiss and all of those other things that are not what we both really want to do. You told me that you've always had mainly physical relationships with women but not since you've been here in Chicago because you've been so busy. I get that. If you've always found them attractive to want to be with them intimately, what is it about me that makes you not want that from me? We make out. You kiss me in a way that I've never experienced before. I know you like me. I know that you want me. What's wrong with me? Is it my background and the things I've done? Am I not the kind of woman that you'd want in that way? I hope that isn't an immature question," she whispered and looked away.

He didn't respond right away. Though he thought taking things a lot slower than he usually would when it came to bedding a woman would be best for them. His thinking that he wanted to make sure he treated her different than how other men have treated her in the past. Just when he assumed he was doing the right thing, he also made her feel like she wasn't worthy of him in an intimate way. That was far from the truth.

"Angel, nothing in this world would give me more pleasure than to make love to you. I can see myself being inside of you for hours and still not get enough. The way we kiss stirs my body up into a frenzy. The number of cold showers I've taken over the past few weeks would probably set some kind of world record. I didn't want what you and I have to be about sex and only sex. I will say, I can't stop thinking about the many times I've had to hold back from initiating sex. I didn't want things to start out with you the way they have always started out with women. When I said I wanted a relationship with you, I meant that. This is new to me. Here I am thinking I'm being a gentleman by keeping my desire for you in check when all along, it seems, I was making you seem like you weren't enough for me to go there with you. Baby, you are more than enough. Every time I touch you, hold you and kiss you, I fight the need to strip us naked and love you until my body conks out from exhaustion. I already know we'll be good together. Don't think you're not enough for me or that I don't want you. I want all of you all the time. I'm talking every day, all day. We all have a past. I'm only interested in the present and the future. I don't want to look back. I don't want you to look back either. There is nothing back there for either one of us."

When her eyes slowly lifted to his, he knew his words had hit home. She'd gotten the confirmation from him that she needed. He wondered what brought this on.

He waited while she reached for her handbag that she'd placed on the floor behind her feet. After she rifled through it, his eyes landed on what was in her hand; a pack of condoms.

"I want you too, Horace. So much so that I bought these recently thinking that we would be taking our relationship to the next level. I've been so ready. Some nights, I can't sleep because all I can think about is the kissing and touching and the so much more of what we haven't been doing. I was starting to think that you didn't want me like that."

Horace undid her seat belt, slid his seat all the way back after making sure the doors were still locked. He turned the car off so that the lights wouldn't be on to show that they were sitting in the car. With all that being checked, he lifted Angel up and placed her in his lap, facing him with her legs on either side of him. He helped her slide her dress further up her legs to be sure she was comfortable. He took the condom from her and put it back in her purse.

He didn't want to talk until he showed her just how aroused she always makes him. It wasn't about the kissing and touching. It was her mere presence that stirred up everyone ion in his body. A wry, sexy grin touched his lips when his eyes focused on hers. Before he kissed her, he did have something to say.

"I've fallen in love with you. Every part of me wants and loves you so much. That revelation hit me fast and hard. I've been holding on to those words for a while now. This moment seems like the perfect time to share that with you. Don't you ever think that you are not the most desirable woman I have ever met. I swear, I saw you and my first thought was the word, forever. What surprised me the most was that I wasn't afraid of that word as I have usually been."

Angel didn't get a chance to respond.

"He kissed her in the most suggestive way possible, making love to her mouth the way he wanted to make love to all of her. Before he placed her back in her seat, he would remove any and all doubt that she's had about herself and about them as a couple. He whispered her name against her lips as he skimmed across them with his tongue. With his hands, he moved her body closer to him, Horace knew the moment she found out for herself, on a physical level, how much he wanted her. She had to feel him. In response, Angel took control of the kiss. She nuzzled and nipped at his lips.

She was igniting a fire in him that burned only for her. As far as he was concerned, his newfound understanding of forever was truly only for her.

"I...I..." Angel started but didn't finish.

"You are a surprise to me; a happy one that I didn't expect."

Horace put a pause between each word for emphasis.

His mouth moved from her lips down to her chin and around to her neck while his hands held onto her hips moving slowly against her.

"You what? You feel me?" he asked.

"*Yyyyyeeesss,* I do," she sighed against his face.

Horace pulled back and locked eyes with her.

"That, sweetheart, is what you always do to me. I've been doing a great job hiding that. You have taught me patience and control. There is nothing wrong with that."

"So, you want to? I mean, I really want to. The way you make me feel always leaves me in a heated state. Um, can I see where you live? Is that okay?"

"That is the best idea I've heard tonight. What about Marlow? Doesn't she have Marleigh? You usually run up to get her when I take you home."

"I'll send her a text. She'll be okay. I don't think we want to be in my apartment tonight. I may yelp like a wild animal. It's been a while for me; not since Marleigh was conceived. Even that, I don't really remember too well. I'm clear and level-headed now. I want to remember everything about us."

Horace kissed her salaciously on the lips one last time before putting her back in her seat. Locking her seat belt and his in place, he turned the car back on and made an illegal U-turn in the middle of the street. He was heading to the Casino

West location where he's been staying since he arrived in Chicago. He leaned over at the next light and kissed her again.

"Thanks for thinking of being safe with the condoms, but I have the ones we'll need at my place. I've been so busy with work since I arrived that the last though I had on my mind was being with anyone. I picked some up the other day, just in case."

She smiled over at him.

"Great, happy minds think alike."

"True, so true. Apparently, so do our amazing desires."

13

Horace parked the car in the owner's secure space under the casino. For the last few miles, they rode in complete silence. The quietness continued as Angel nervously stood next to him on the elevator as it rose to the top floor where there were only two suites. One belonged to Torrence, which he and Reese sometimes used, but mostly he kept it for special friends and guests. The other was his. Though he had stayed in it once before, right after the casino opened, he hadn't been in it again until he moved to Chicago. To him, it was more of an apartment or condo than a hotel suite. Unlike other suites, the space was comprised of all furniture that he purchased. The design was nothing like the other suites. Every room had his personal touch thanks to a friend of Reese's who was an interior designer.

When the doors opened on his floor, they still hadn't said more than a few words. Anxiety had clearly gotten a hold of them together and individually. He could hear Angel's high heels clicking on the hardwood floors in order to keep up with his long strides. He wanted to apologize for his hurried nature. It was the excitement of being along to love all on her the way he'd been dreaming of doing since the beginning. By the time they reached the door, Angel was laughing. He turned to her before he got the door opened by entering. Curiosity ha definitely gotten a hold of him.

"Do you want to let me in on the joke?"

"I think we are both extra excited. Did you realize how fast you have been walking since we got out of the car? I'm exhausted just from walking down this hallway."

That caused him to laugh too.

"All this kiss and sex talk had me ready to pick you up and slide inside of you in the elevator. I had to fight that feeling with everything in me. Don't laugh baby. We were close to that happening," he said before blowing her a kiss and unlocking his door. "I'll give you the code before I take you home in the morning. I want you to be here anytime you want. I'll make sure hotel and casino security know to let you right up. I want to be sure they all know who you are on sight."

Once inside, Angel looked around at the massive space once he flipped a switch and every light in the large room lit up.

"You have a thing for black and gold, I see. It's not just at the casino. Rhonda took each applicant on a tour during the interview. She wanted us to see what we were working for; the casino, not the owners. If I thought that was magnificent, that was before seeing your place. I love it. This is all custom-made?"

"Yes. I picked out everything you see here."

Angel walked over to the window that allowed her to look out over the bright Chicago lights.

"I've never seen a view like this. You get to see this every night?"

"Yes, baby. Yes, I do. You can see it too, as often as you want to. My place is your place."

There was something in the way he responded that made her turn around. He knew why.

"I said that to you. I remember that day. I think it was that day I saw you having a heated conversation in your truck."

"You saw that?"

"I did."

"You didn't say anything."

"I didn't want to pry."

"You could never pry. I'm an open book. That day, I had been talking to a woman I had been physically involved with."

"I figured it was a woman."

"It was. It was the end of what we'd had going on. She wasn't happy about it. I wanted to be free to be with you like that time for us and now."

"Even then, you knew?"

"From day one, I knew. There were so many stolen moments with you. Can I say what my favorite was?"

Angel nodded.

"One day I want to hear them all. For now, yes, I want to hear your favorite."

"Parking my car and seeing you sitting in the window as if you were waiting for me. I know I was coming by to work on the house, but that moment, every single time. I would see you and wonder if we could have something. I thought about the kind of man I want to be for you. We've both had a rough life. That didn't mean we didn't deserve each other. Seeing you in the window like that had me determined that I wanted you to see me. I mean, really see me."

"I saw you then. I see you now. I'm different when I see you. I want to be the kind of woman that you would want. I've never cared about that before. I care about you."

"That is mutual, baby."

"Why are you so fine?"

"I could ask you the same question, Ms. Angel. We would be here all night with the number of reasons I can come up with to compliment you. I surely don't want to rush the night but, come here, baby."

Horace opened his arms to her. Angel ran right into them. When he lifted her into his arms and kissed her like a starving man, she went with the flow. She wrapped her legs around his waist and her arms around his neck, stirring up fiery embers of a need he'd never felt before. That's saying something for a man with a past that included more women than he'd ever tell anyone about other than his best friend.

"Horace," she murmured eagerly against his lips.

"I know, baby. Me too," he replied before walking them across the room and down the hall to the master bedroom.

Lights automatically illuminated the room. Horace hit a switch on the wall and the room was again covered in darkness. When they reached the bed, he placed his hand over a button on the wall and soft lighting came at them from all corners of the room. Something told her to look up. When she did, she marveled at what she saw. There was a skylight above the bed that let in a perfect view of the starry and now, romantic night.

"The views are something to magnetic. I can't believe this is you every night."

"Well, it can be you anytime you want. Feel free to bring Marleigh when you can do that. We'll make a space for her that's all hers in the guest room. I know you come as a package deal."

"You don't mind?"

"Never, ever will I mind. I love every part of you and that includes your daughter."

"Horace, I love you too. I want you to know that. I thought I've been in love before but you've shown me what I experienced before you cannot compare to real, true love that I've found in your arms."

Horace slid her body down his. He took her small purse from her hand and opened it, retrieving her cell phone.

"Call Marlow before you forget. I don't want her to think something happened to you."

"Okay. Can I use your bathroom?"

"There is one through the walk-in closet. There is also one in the hall. We walked past it on our way to the bedroom."

"Yeah, I missed that. I was otherwise occupied by your lips." You know I can't think when you kiss me.

Once inside, she closed the door and called Marlow, who answered on the first ring.

"Are you calling to tell me you won't be home tonight?" she asked before Angel could get even one word out.

"What are you a mind reader or something? Anyway, are you okay with that? I'll come home if you need me to. I'm at Horace's place. I'm planning to spend the night here unless you need me to come get Marleigh."

"Are you insane? You want to trade a night with your man for an evening of bottles and diaper changes? Be real, sis."

Angel hit her own self softly on the side of her head and then laughed about it.

"I'll be there in the morning. Horace can drop me off on his way to work."

"Have fun, baby sis. Remember, you deserve to be this happy. The house alarm is on and I'm about to facetime Joey for some sexy time with him now that the girls are bathed and in their beds in the nursery. I'll kiss Marleigh for you."

"Thanks. I appreciate you. I'll see you in the morning."

Ending the call, she moved to the mirror and gave herself a once-over. Tonight was the night, she thought. She's been wanting this. It appears, so has Horace. To show him just how ready she was, she slipped out of her dress which left her standing in her heels, high-cut lace panties and a demi-cup bra, all in black, that barely held in her breasts. She removed the band that held her hair up above her head. When her long tresses fell around her shoulders, she fixed it just the way she wanted so that encircled her face. Turning to look at herself from behind, she smiled at the satisfaction she felt. Grabbing her things, she headed back to the bedroom, dropping her dress right inside of the door.

Horace was in front of her with his back to her while he connected his phone to his audio system. She waited with her hands on her hips in her heels and panties and waited until he noticed that she had returned. She didn't have to wait long.

"My god, woman. Are you trying to give me a heart attack? Wow! That's what's been under that dress all-night? You are stunning in and out of everything."

She didn't speak. She kept her eyes on his every move. Horace wasted no time removing his shirt, shoes and pants. She delighted at the sight of him in black and gold boxer briefs; or at least most of him. There was a part of him that peaked out over the top because it was clear, all of him couldn't fit in the material. Gold pack indeed, her head shouted.

He moved in her direction at the same time that she moved closer to him. They met in the middle at the edge of the bed. She was vividly imagining him with nothing on. She didn't have to wait long. Before she could reach to help him remove the last of his clothing, he slid the boxers down to the floor. When he reached for her, she moved with certainty of what she wanted; *him*. She wanted him.

Their need for each other could be heard in the only sound in the room – their feathered breathing.

Horace lifted her up and turned so that her back was to the bed. He laid her down. Covering her body with his, being skin-to-skin, sent his desire surging skyward.

Angel was having a moment that was quite foreign to her. Heat flashed keenly through her bones, stimulating her flesh with a nuance of need. When is lips found hers, she sighed into the kiss. To say that she was happy that she was finally where she wanted and needed to be was not an exaggeration.

When his hand caressed her face before sliding down to caress her breasts through the material covering them, she waited with anticipation as he moved one cup to the side and caressed her nipple. Another stream of heat spanned from her eyes to where his lips now replaced his hand over her breast. She whimpered her delight when he slid the other cup down and went between the large mounds.

She couldn't keep her hips still. They seemed to move in a circular position on their own, encourage him to continue on. She rested her hands on his shoulders as he moved further down her body. His tongue ravished her from one side to the other. She shifted a little to give him room to unsnap her bra from behind her. When the cups fell away, he tossed it to the floor and continued his kissing down the center of her body.

Her breath stalled in her throat. She closed her eyes and enjoyed the feel of being loved by the man she loved. The idea of that thrilled her. She was thankful for whatever in was responsible for sending a man like him her way.

Horace turned her body slightly to the side. He gripped the edge of her panties with his teeth. When he sucked on her hip, her body shot up off the bed. That little nip seared sexily to every part of her body, first simmering heat, now a full-fledged flame.

She wasn't sure she could take much more without turning their bodies, placing hers on top and taking control of the pace.

Nothing could describe how much she wanted him to get her to the sexual release she was imagining and craving.

Horace slid her panties from her body. Angel's brain screamed for more when he spread her legs and slid into the space between them. While his hands continued to caress her body, moving back up to her breasts, she sucked in a breath the moment his mouth found its way to the sensitive space between her legs. She'd never been one to enjoy oral pleasure. Now she knew why. No one had ever caused her body to sing. The way Horace's tongue slowly lapped at her, she opened her legs wider to give him more room to drive her wilder.

Angel couldn't stop her head from thrashing about from side to side even if she tried. Horace feasted on her. The soft lighting in the room allowed her to see him in action. The vision in front of her was of his mouth loving her in small circles. Horace's eyes planted squarely on hers. His smokey look teased and tantalized her. She pushed her hips toward his mouth. Her moans escaped and filled the air in the room. She sucked in her breath and held on for the wild ride.

"Yes!" Horace's raspy voice coaxed her.

Her body shattered quickly and without warning. She begged and pleaded for more. His fingers caressed her hard nipples, rolling them from the tips of his fingers to the *V* of them. His mouth going between nipping at her and lapping at her prolonged the orgasm that tore through her like a raging rocket. She saw stars. As much as she tried to contain her yells of pleasure, she couldn't when her mouth opened and she heard her own screams of gratification bouncing off of the walls.

She was still riding out her pleasure when Horace replaced his lips with his pleasure-seeking fingers. He must be multi-tasking, she thought. Somewhere in the midst of her body thrashing about, he'd reached for a condom. She heard him tearing it open with his teeth. That was when she opened her eyes to see what his other hand was doing because one hand was still between her legs, caressing her, causing her desire for him to stir up again, quickly.

Taking a moment to protect them with the condom in place, Horace covered her body, focusing on his lips covering hers.

Angel could taste the sweetness of her own body on his lips. She was thirsty for him.

She'd never experienced such a thing before. The feel of him, the taste of her and the smell of him together had every part of her on full-alert. When his manhood grazed her inner thigh, she held her breath in anticipation of what was to come.

Angel opened her legs wider when he placed each of her legs in the crook of his arms before reaching between them to guide himself into her body. His eyes never left hers.

"You see me, baby," he uttered against her lips.

He moved into her body a little at a time.

"Yes, yes," she moaned in pleasure.

"Do you feel me?" he crooned against the side of her face near her ear.

"Yes, baby, I feel you. You feel like heaven."

When Horace slid inside of her, grinding his hips forward before retreating and pulling out until only the tip remained, his world collided with his heart.

When Horace slid slowly back in, giving her more of him, Angel opened her eyes and saw the strain on his face. He was holding back from going in all the way. He was snug inside of her. Angel didn't care. She wanted every delicious inch.

"My goodness, you feel good, slippering and soaking wet," Horace moaned.

A wicked grin graced Angel's face. This man she loved was finally hers.

When Horace clicked his tongue across her lips and played with her tongue, chasing after it in a lovingly, playful manner, she joined in their loving, pumping her hips, meeting him stroke for stroke. When he switched to a circular, more penetrating motion, Angel practically howled with thanks.

With her legs up in the air, Angel looked down at the same time that Horace did. She was able to see what was behind his large, thick and powerful strokes. She kept her eyes on his movements until her body rose to claim all of her again with another strong, desperate surge, bringing them closer together; from heart-to-heart.

Horace knew she was close. He pulled back and focused on her face. Her orgasm took over and her head flew back as she wailed like a wild she-devil into the air around them. With increased strokes in and out of her body, the sounds of their love making pierced the air around them.

With a growl, Horace orgasmed with a fierce roar that masterfully encased him in a haze of determined love and passion.

Angel felt her body floating to a whole new level, not known to her.

They rode out the pleasure together.

It seemed like an eternity before their body's calmed enough that would allow any semblance of speech from either of them. The air was still filled with their heavy breathing. Angel focused all of her attention on the sounds of Horace kissing her lips, to her face, to her arms and then to her breasts where he laid his head between them and let go of a relaxed sigh. She caressed his body to soothe him after he put in the work of focusing all of his attention on pleasing her.

After another slow lick across her chest, he leaned up on his elbows and kissed her sweetly on the forehead. Angel closed her eyes and enjoyed the lingering feel of him there.

"You will always be worth the wait. For starters, you are just so damned beautiful, especially now, post all of that. I'm not sure there is any blood left in the other parts of my body. I'm content with laying here, if you don't mind."

Angel kissed his forehead again and again.

"I could lay like this forever. If there wasn't a life outside of this room, I could really do that."

"You're mine, Angel. I hope you're ready for being all mine. In turn, no one will ever be able to claim me but you. We are in this together, yes?" he asked.

Leaning down to kiss his waiting lips, she shook her head yes. She was too overwhelmed with the feeling of the most powerful feeling of love, lust and fulfillment. He was definitely all hers.

"You and me. I'm with whatever and everything that looks like.

14

The feeling of being in love brought out other feelings that Horace wasn't prepared for. He was starting to question his decision to stay away from his family all of these years. What he wanted to do was find a way to build a bridge to connect with them again. Sure, he and his sisters texted and talked a few times a year. That wasn't enough; not anymore. What set his mind on this path was the events of the day before.

A month after he and Angel sealed their love with a night and morning of amazing sex, he spent several nights with her at her apartment. That had been his first time staying over. He did something that he was learning to do more and more; he left work early to relax with her and Marleigh. Best of all, he turned off his cell phone so that they had his undivided attention. Torrence put him onto remembering that they had a competent staff in place so that they could step back.

The next week, Angel called after work and said she was on her way to his place. She told him not to rush home from work because she would be there when he got off. While he appreciated the way she put him first, he canceled one meeting and pushed another one to the next day. He still didn't get to her until eight that night. Instead of staying in, they went down to the casino and spent some time playing the slot machines. That was a first for Angel. Things didn't go her way often.

She didn't win big today. She did, however, come away with more than what she started with. A win is a win.

They then had fun at the night club before ordering a late-night dinner to be delivered to his apartment. As much as they both wanted to make love, they didn't. Instead, the night was spent sharing more about what they like and didn't like in life. They talked until they fell asleep on the sofa together. When he suddenly woke around two in the morning, he picked Angel up and carried her to bed. Quality time like this is something he didn't share with any other woman before. Angel was special. Her name alone gave him hope that what they were sharing would bring them a lifetime of love.

His greatest pleasure came the day before when Angel finally had her day in family court. The date had been changed a few times. She was able to prove to the judge that she was on the right path. She was allowed her to speak on her own behalf instead of through her attorney.

In the two months since everything had happened, she has since enrolled in community college part-time, taking classes online at her own pace. She was employed full-time at the casino with her first day starting on Monday, in three days. She spoke of how her sister and the rest of her family have become her rock. She also spoke of her love for him, which surprised everyone. He came along to her hearing as support. Sitting in the back of the room with Marlow, her brother and several of their friends. He spent most of the time holding Marleigh. Angel had her at the start of the hearing. When she saw him over Angel's shoulder, all she wanted was for him to pick her up. He tried distracting her with funny faces and waves, but that wasn't enough. Even the judge noticed her penchant for only wanting Horace to hold her. In a wild move, he interrupted the hearing when Marleigh began to cry. He suggested that maybe for the moment, Angel hand Marleigh over to him.

The minute he walked up and picked Marleigh up from Angel's arms, she stopped crying and began to giggle at everyone else. When he sat down, she quieted, took her bottle and fell asleep almost immediately. There was no way the proceedings were going to move forward without her explaining what they'd all just seen.

She told the court that she'd fallen in love with a wonderful man who loved her and her daughter. She noted that as everyone could see, her daughter was just as smitten with the love of her life as she was. She talked about the fun they had together and how he was the one who fixed up her apartment; the one that child services were proud of. It was shared that her legal matters were behind her with all of those charges dropped. The child services team gave her a raving recommendation that all restrictions be removed and Marleigh be returned to her. At the end, Marlow also spoke about all the changes Angel had made so that she and her daughter could have a better life. For the time being, they would continue to live with her until one day when Angel felt comfortable enough to make the step toward living completely on her own.

In the end, the judge removed every restriction and ordered that sole custody be returned to Angel. He wished her well and said he had a feeling that he would never see her in his courtroom again.

Angel had yelled, never, and the entire courtroom cheered for her, including the judge. She felt like a celebrity. Putting herself and her daughter first was the answer.

Their intimate life had only grown stronger and wilder since that first night. Now that she could take Marleigh wherever she wanted without having to have Marlow in tow, they were planning for her and Marleigh to spend the night at his place. Knowing that, he'd gone out around noon to purchase the same crib that Angel had for Marleigh at her apartment. He didn't want her to have to travel with too much when it was time for them to come to his place. Rhonda had given all of the new employees their last Friday off in order for them to prepare for their regular schedules after the weekend.

For their first night all together, he was going to make them a pot of spaghetti to celebrate the freedom Angel was given.

Thinking about her and Marleigh, he reached for his phone before he hustled off to his last meeting of the afternoon. Starting next week, he would be moving around on roller skates from one end of the day to the other. Angel knew that their time would be limited so they talked about either he would spend the night at her place when he was done or her and Marleigh would prepare to spend the night at his place until he came home. He loved going to bed with her in his arms. He'd even come to enjoy giving Marleigh her last bottle of the night before she went down. He never thought that this would be his life. He was building a family. It was time he connected with his own. Before calling Angel, he dialed Liza. This was her work study day.

"What's wrong?" Liza questioned.

He didn't get a chance to say hello.

"Whoa there, cowgirl. Who said anything was wrong?"

"You never call. You always text to say hello. If you're calling, I assumed there was an issue. Are you okay?"

"I'm fine and no, nothing is wrong. I was thinking about you and Lisa. I thought I'd see what you thought about me coming for a visit soon."

"Brother, don't make me go crazy up in here, up in *here*! You're playing with me, right? You really want to come for a visit? You've never done that. Lisa and I have been begging you for years to come see us or let us come see you in Las Vegas or Chicago now, or wherever you are. Where are you?"

He laughed. His sisters kept him humble and in check.

"I'm in Chicago which is where I plan to live. The new casino is opening soon. I sent you pictures of the construction. It's pretty much all done. We're in the middle of plans for the grand opening."

"Can we come? I know it's not happening right away. Can we come if mommy says we can? You texted a month ago that kids under eighteen can come for the party. We just can't come into the casino. I've never been to an event like. This little town doesn't have anything going on like that. I've seen some stuff on social media about big-time parties. A lot is on social media about your casino. The country is trying to come. I hear you will have Rihanna in the house. I'm still trying to convince mommy to let me get some of her lingerie. She says I'm not old enough yet."

"She's right. That stuff is not for my baby sisters. You are not ready for that. I'm not ready for you to have that."

"Hmph. I bet you buy that kind of stuff for all those women you are always seen with. I know they like that stuff. Some of them wear it like an outfit."

"Liza, stop it. I'm not seen with a bunch of women; at least not anymore. I'm in a relationship with a very beautiful woman named Angel."

"Wait, did you say relationship? You're in love?"

"Yes, I am. I want you and Lisa to meet her and her daughter. I actually want our mother to meet her as well."

When Liza got quiet, he gave her a minute before questioning why.

"She has a baby?"

"You're quiet little sister. You good? Yes, she has a daughter and she's as beautiful as her mother."

"I'm good. You're going to make mommy happy. She's always asking about you through us. I think she tries to keep up with you on social media. She's always asking me or Lisa how to find stuff about you. It's time for you to talk to her directly. She would love to hear from you. She understands the trauma you experienced as a kid. She's been going through counseling and it has helped. Daddy isn't a good man. He will never change. We know that now. Lisa and I are good with the distance he has decided to create between us. Mommy is a lot happier. She has a lot of guilt over how you left and never came back other than to ask to be emancipated from them. She told us she only said yes because she didn't want daddy to drag you down like he did Prince. She wanted you away from him, just not away from her."

Horace didn't know his sisters knew. Anytime they talk, that isn't a subject that comes up. He wants his family around. That means visiting old demons and putting them to rest. That means confronting his mother to clear the air. The unconditional love Angel and Marleigh gave him only had him wanting to lay eyes on and hug his own family. He didn't understand that kind of love until he fell in love. Now, he knew the kind of feelings that weren't shared with him as a child. These new feelings are what he had always been missing.

"I didn't know she told you about that. It was a bad time in our lives after Prince died. I felt like I, like daddy, let him down instead of helping him."

"You were sixteen. That's too much weight for anyone to carry, especially my brother. Mommy says that all the time. I'm so happy you called. When are you thinking of visiting? Can you talk to mommy about us coming for the grand opening party?"

"I don't know exactly when I'll visit. I doubt it's before the opening of the casino. There is so much that needs to be done. If she says you and Lisa can come, I will fly you out and put you in a suite. There will be rules, of course. I'm sure my girlfriend would love to take you shopping for something to wear."

"Something by a designer? You know mommy doesn't spend money on that stuff."

"Yes, something designer. Whatever you want. She has to agree to it before we do any of that. I have to make a few calls before a meeting. Why don't you call me later from the house. I can hear from the background that you're not home. With all three of you on the phone, let's talk about some stuff. I'm thinking around seven tonight? Is that good?"

"It will be. I'm glad you called. I love you, big brother. I don't know if you hear those words often, but I really love you. I can't wait to see you."

"I love you too, munchkin. Tell Lisa, I love her."

He hesitated and didn't send the same sentiment to his mother. They had some work to do in order to get to that point.

"I will."

His next call was to Angel. When she didn't answer, he was leaving her a voicemail message when she called.

"Hey beautiful. I was just leaving you a message. I didn't want anything. I just wanted to call and say I love you. How is your day?"

"Perfect now. I was just finishing packing Marleigh's bag for the weekend at your place. We're going to come home Sunday evening so that she's already here for Marlow when I leave for work. I want to get there bright and early."

"Will I get the chance to drive you to work?"

"No, Horace. I'm going to take a rideshare. I do need to get my driver's license. Joey's friend, Carter said he would give Joey a good price on a car for me.

"That's nice of him."

"You're still taking me driving, right?"

"Anything for you. What time will you and Marleigh be ready? I'll swing by and pick you up. I'm also making it a short day. Monday will be crazy. That's another reason why I'm giving myself a break this weekend. I can't wait to spend it spoiling my two favorite people."

"We should be ready around six. Does that work?"

"Yes."

"I want to take Marleigh out for a walk down to the park a few blocks away. It's a nice, warm day out. The fact that I don't have to have anyone's permission to spend quiet time out with my daughter is a kind of freedom I didn't know I needed in my life. Marlow is happy too. She and Joey took Maia to see his sister."

"I bet Marleigh will love being out with just you. Will Marlow be back before you leave?"

"No. I think they plan on hanging over Alyssa's house into the evening. There is an electrician coming here at four. I told her I would be here to let him in. Before you worry, don't. It's someone who is friends with Joey and Carlos. He shouldn't be here long."

"Okay, I'll let you get to that. I need to stop at the store to pick up a few last-minute things. Do you have everything you need for the baby? I have the crib. I just need to put it together when I get home. I also picked up some toys and some other stuff for her. Don't forget her elephant. I would get her another one but I think she would know the difference if it wasn't that exact one."

"You're right. I think I'm good."

"Okay. Sounds good."

"We can Instacart for anything else that may come up once I get there. I love you. I'll call you when we get back from the park."

"Okay, be careful. Don't forget, the hotel has a small convenience store. I love you too."

His call ended just as his assistant entered his office to remind him that he has a meeting in the main conference room. He went on his way with an extra swagger to his walk. It was the walk of a man who was happier in his life than he has ever been.

15

Angel locked her door and carried Marleigh on one hip while she grabbed the stroller with her other hand. She checked to be sure she had her phone, key and Marleigh's bag before strapping her in to begin their walk. They had only gone a short distance when her phone rang. It was Kris. Putting her ear pods in her ear, she started down the street, waving at neighbors who were probably shocked to see her out and about. Most only saw her coming and leaving. She was more than ready to enjoy the community and meet some neighbors.

"Hey Kris. How are you?"

"I'm good. I was calling to check in on you. I know our business is done, but I wanted to have one last conversation to be sure you're all set."

"Oh, yes. I'm good. The criminal case is done and the family court issues are all resolved. Marleigh and I are living our best life. We're about to take a nice walk to the park. Did you hear that? I'm taking my own walk out in public with my daughter and no one else. It feels amazing. I feel amazing. Thank you for your help with everything. You are truly a lifesaver."

"Angel, you did the work. You get the credit. Everyone stumbles a time or two. The idea is to get back up again and again. You are worth it and so is your little girl. Listen, I need to ask you something that's been on my mind. That cop, Charlie, have you heard anything from him?"

"No. Why would I hear from him? He doesn't know how to reach me. That phone I had, I don't have anymore. I have a new number. Why would he want to reach out to me. I'm sure he hates me for blowing up his life."

"Exactly. I'm concerned. I heard from a friend of mine that he's been spiraling out of control after the inquiring from internal affairs led to his suspension. I was told he was officially fired from the force earlier this week. My friend called to tell me that he was ranting and raving about how you ruined his life. I just want you to be careful. Men like him whose lives have been destroyed can be vindictive. She said he also talked about how you were able to walk away without any repercussions while he was fired. His wife tossed him out. They have friends in common who say he's not himself these days."

"I haven't heard anything. I don't even think about him anymore. That trauma is behind me. I've been doing good. I officially start my job on Monday. I'm in love and enjoying all the new changes in my life. The last thing I want to do is revisit any issues that involve Charlie. Him and everything about him is behind me. I do need to get the final court papers. Do you have them? I think you mentioned everything would be sent directly to you."

"I'm working on that package now. I'll probably stop by one day next week to drop everything off with you. Besides, I want to see your little lady. She is the cutest little one with that head full of long, thick hair. She's not even a year old yet. She's close though I think."

"She is. Marlow and I are going to throw her a party next week. I hope you can come. There is a party room as a part of the daycare center next to the new casino. We're going to rent that out along with the area outside. There is equipment for kids to play one. We're also renting one of those bounce houses. We have to get it all planned out. Horace is working on getting a cleaning crew to come in on the morning of the party to sanitize all of the equipment. He said the center, which is owned by the casino, already does that each evening. For private events, the person using it has to pay for that themselves. I'm more than happy to do that."

"I will make sure I'm there. Just text me all the information when you have it. Listen, just be careful and watch your surroundings. I don't think he's out to get you. If you happen to run into him anywhere, go the other way and don't engage. If you feel threatened, call the police. This will die down. Charlie will find something else to do in life besides blame you for his downfall. He brought it on himself just like his commander told us. Especially since he was in uniform."

Angel shook off the stench that was Charlie. She was happy that all of that bad stuff was behind her. She was out with her daughter. Tonight, she would be in the arms of her man. Life was perfect.

"Some people are just creeps. He is one of those people. His wife deserves better. I finally realized that I deserved better than what I was doing to myself. I have Horace and I'm good. I appreciate the call. I better get off of here and focus on the walk. There are a lot of people out and about."

"Alright, take care. Call me if you need me for anything."

"I will. Thanks again, Kris."

Angel took her buds out of her ears and checked on Marleigh. With her few teeth gleaming in the daylight, Marleigh's eyes went from one person who walked by and waved to the next.

Seeing the park ahead on the other side of the street, she stood at the curb and waited for the light to change. She wasn't focused on anything other than making sure she watched the stoplight to get across the street on time.

**

There she was. Charlie felt a tinge of satisfaction knowing that he'd finally caught her out by herself. She wasn't exactly alone, but she was alone enough for him. He didn't care anything about her kid. It was her he was out to get.

He had been scoping out her house for days. He got heated every time he saw her with a man, he assumed was her new man. The guy seemed to be pretty well off. He looked familiar but didn't know why that was so. He didn't care. His attention was on Angel. He'd had nothing but payback on his mind since internal affairs investigated him. They determined that he was a detriment to himself and the department. It wasn't just Angel who had tanked his life, but she was cause. Because of her, his activities with other women surfaced. Even his friends on the force had turned their backs on him. He was reduced to just another bum out in the world. He didn't care about anything anymore. Nothing mattered other than revenge.

Driving down the road at a slow pace, he followed Angel to see where she was going. He didn't have a plan in mind other than to make her feel his pain in any way possible. She was yet another woman who played with him.

He thought she was into what he had in mind for her. All he wanted was a little fun with her cute, sexy body. From the few talks they'd had when he admittedly stalked her, he learned of her checkered past. That had him thinking she would be down for whatever he had in mind. Where she got the courage to go against him like she did as he was driving them out of town to his usual hotel, he didn't know. What he did know what he was tired of women like her who flaunted their beauty and then turned it off like a switch. He wasn't for that now and wouldn't be again.

For a second, he lost sight of her pushing her daughter in the stroller when they stopped at the light. There were other people in his line of sight to her. He thought that she would keep straight and cross the road ahead of her. Instead, she was looking to walk across traffic right in front of him. He banged his fist on the steering wheel, wishing he was the first car. He could clear his mind and push his foot on the pedal when the light changed. What happened after that, he wouldn't care. He could keep driving with no destination in mind. His revenge would be sweet. The problem was, he couldn't get to her. Not only was there a car in front of him, but there were a lot of people, especially children, crossing the street in the same direction. That wasn't the chance he was hoping for. If he ran into her, there would be a lot more carnage than he had hoped for.

Charlie kept his eyes focused on her. Even in his anger, she was still beautiful and desirous. With everything that she'd done, he still wanted her. Despite that, he couldn't let her get away with what she'd done to him. He would bide his time and come for her when the time was right. That wasn't right now.

When the light finally changed and the car ahead of him moved, he sat still with his gaze focused on her. He was sickened by the way she moved through life all happy and pleased with her life while his was trash; pure trash. He has lost the respect of everyone he knows because of her.

When the car behind him honked, he moved on, slowing down when he got close to her. He didn't think she could see him with the dark windows. If he could get closer to do what he was feigning to do, he would want her to know that it was him. He was also in a different car than his unmarked patrol car she was used to seeing him in.

He kept driving until she was no longer in sight. There would be another time. That he knew was a sure thing.

16

Putting Marleigh to bed had become something Horace looked forward to anytime he and Angel spent the night together. His heart grew three sizes every time Marleigh's toothy grin hit him with more love than he ever thought he'd get from anyone.

After picking them up for the weekend at Angel's apartment, they had gone for a car ride to enjoy the early evening before he finally pulled into the parking garage of the casino. He'd helped Angel get Marleigh out of the back before grabbing the bags of items he'd picked up from the store before picking them up. The whole moment felt domesticated. The old Horace would have run for the hills to get away from it. Who he was now welcomed and embraced times like this.

After Angel opened the stroller, he placed Marleigh in it and they headed for the garage elevator with him pushing it. Horace chuckled to himself thinking about how he looked pushing a baby stroller. They moved together as if they'd been together for years.

Once inside of his place, he got right to putting Marleigh's crib together while Angel put everything away and kept the baby entertained. Even Angel was surprised when he said he'd like to keep the stroller up and in the spare room even after the weekend. He wanted to officially declare what was his guestroom to now be her room away from home. When Angel kissed him and told him how much she loved that idea, he was happy because she was. Anyone on the outside looking at them may say that things were moving too fast between them. He would respond that his heart led him here. His heart would keep him here and going full speed ahead.

More than anything, he wanted Angel to see them as a family. He didn't want it any other way. That's the direction they were heading in.

"You're really off for the entire weekend? No plans?"

Angel addressed him after he closed the door to Marleigh's room and joined her on the sofa in front of the television. He had peeped into the kitchen where they had eaten dinner. He couldn't believe that he had looked at the same floor that he'd seen before Angel had given Marleigh her bath. The baby had decorated the floor with spaghetti noodles and sauce. It was back to the clean, light gray wood floors, pre-spaghetti. He was prepared to clean it up after putting Marleigh to bed. Angel had beat him to it.

While he handled the baby, Angel had cleaned up the kitchen after they ate dinner, especially the nice floor design Marleigh made with her spaghetti noodles. He was tickled and took a picture of her creative design. Who was he, he questioned? He had easily fallen into father mode.

"All of my attention is for the two of you this weekend. I don't know when we'll get three straight days of peace and quiet without either of the casinos or hotels coming into play with one issue here and there. I want to enjoy this time for what it is."

"Is Marleigh good and sleep? Sometimes, she can fake sleep. Five minutes after putting her down, she'll be up and crying to be let out of her crib."

"She is very much asleep. She took the entire bottle. She sat quietly in my lap sipping on it while I read her a story. When that bottle fell out of her little hands, that was the only signal I needed to put her down. It's you who likes to hold her for an hour after she'd down."

"Horace, I'm getting better at that. Now that life has some normalcy to it, I know that my time with her alone isn't limited. She sure did love that spaghetti. A lot of it ended up on the floor. She ate more than I thought she would."

"She's like her mother. She loves to eat. I don't know how you have this perfect coke soda bottle figure with the way you throw down. I do love a woman who is a healthy eater."

Angel turned to him with a questionable look.

"There have been other women that you love?"

"You know better than to ask me that. You took my cherry when it comes to this love thing, baby. Speaking of cherries, that lip gloss you had on earlier was delicious."

Horace licked his lips to give the proper impact while she was gazing at him. When her eyes went to his lips, his head screamed, *jackpot!*

"Must have been. Somebody kissed all of it off of me."

"Well, if you were wearing any now, I would do that again. I enjoy kissing you. I love how your lips have that thoroughly kissed look when I'm done."

"Is that all?"

"All what? Kissing you? Again, you know the answer to that, so why even ask," he retorted lightheartedly.

"I can go put some on if you want me to. I brought it with me."

When she attempted to get up, Horace pulled her back onto his lap. He held her there with her back to him. He took that opportunity to kiss all of the exposed skin around her neck that he could reach, first with his lips and then with his tongue. Even though he'd seen her through the week, tonight was different.

"You look sexy when you were my shirts. They look more like a dress on you."

Moving his hands up her body under the inside front of the shirt, his heart skipped a beat when he found that underneath, she only had on a pair of panties. He rubbed all around the barely there string material. He loved all of her. They were both already aware that he was obsessed with her behind. He gripped both cheeks, wiggling them in his hands.

"Damn, you have on a thong. I love them," he murmured against the back of her neck.

He was dressed in a pair of silk pajama bottoms and a white t-shirt. Being nude was his usual attire when he was home alone. Having Marleigh with them, he changed up.

When Angel started sliding around on his lap due to the soft, slipperiness of the material he had on, he moved his hips around with her. He let his hands wander up across her bare chest, loving the feel of her breasts which were bare for his pleasure. Any time he got a chance to freely touch her without an audience, he wanted his hands on all of her.

"Don't start something unless your follow-through game is on point."

Angel spoke to him over her shoulder, leaning back and squirming around. When she bent forward and twerked on him, Horace held on and watched her move. Her tease game was fire. He was being controlled by the sway of her hips and the connection of their hearts.

"Oh, is this a challenge? You know everything about my game is ready for you. I have what you want and need at any time, night or day."

In a swift move of her hips, Angel turned around on his lap, putting her body in one of his favorite positions. Having her straddle him gave him an immediate rise for what he had planned for the rest of the evening.

"It's a promise, baby," Angel replied with gusto as she leaned down to sample his lips.

When the quick pecks weren't enough, he held her head to his and laved her mouth with penetrating tonguing, just the way she loved. Their affection for each other could never be denied. They moved together as out and especially, in bed.

Horace smiled and laughed against her lips when she reached down and pulled his shirt up and over her head, tossing it to the floor. His eyes followed her hands as they traveled up and down his body; especially down and then further down even more.

When her hand reached that part of him that pointed up and, in her direction, Horace had to grit his teeth to keep from turning her over and sliding into her out of sheer untamed passion.

"Baby, you know what I need to get before we turn the heat up as high as you want."

"Do you? We were tested twice. Do you remember why?" she leaned back and asked.

"You're good now?"

Never in his life had he ever had sex with a woman without a condom. If what she was insinuating was true, he was about to. He was more than ready.

"I've been on birth control for over a month now. I can get a condom if you want one. You know I'm all about that. I know we talked about the next level, which is no barrier, as long as we were tested and I was on birth control. I know we don't want any children," she noted.

Horace thought about his response. He was shocked that he was about to say it, but he did.

"Right now."

"Huh?" Angel questioned.

"Right now. We don't want any kids right now. We have a lifetime of being together. We will want kids when we're ready."

"Mmm," she murmured against his lips. "Yes, one day."

Solidifying that they were on the same page, Horace lifted his hands in surrender. He didn't dare fight her when she reached inside of his pajama pants and pulled out that part of him that love being inside of her. With both hands, she stroked him from top to bottom. Him being ready didn't take much other than her wicked contemplation of what she was ready to bring to the night. Her beauty turned him on in an instant.

"I want to ride," she whispered against his lips, nipping lightly at first the top and then the bottom.

"Come on, baby. Do you. I'm always down for a good, sexy ride. You do it so well!" he declared breathlessly.

Angel didn't need any more coaxing from him. He placed his hands behind him on top of the sofa and held on. She loved doing the work when they were in this position.

When she steadied herself over him, he moved his hands to her ass and moved her thong to the side. He easily moved inside of her and lost the ability to breathe at the smooth, inviting feel of her feminine walls milking him. He'd never felt what it was like being inside of a woman without a barrier. He had definitely been missing out not falling in love with the right woman before Angel. Still, he was glad he hadn't. That would have meant that he wouldn't have her and Marleigh. That would have been a true tragedy.

"This feels so different to actually feel you," she uttered against his lips.

Horace held her body in his hands. Helping her set a zealous pace, going up and down on him, slow at first and then faster when she picked up the pace to truly him like a cowgirl. That was his nickname for her. She loved it and now he knew why he did as well.

"Amazing," he slurred out, watching her hips move all around him. "You feel wonderful, just like I knew you would when we came together, flesh to flesh."

"That's because I'm yours and you are mine, right?"

Horace nodded. He never wanted her to have any doubts about them.

"Forever and always, my love."

Angel gripped his shoulders and took them to the top until they moaned out their mutual reverberating, low erotogenic, enticingly purrs. Sending his love juices up inside of her and feeling her essence milking all around him, had him roaring like a lion.

His body, especially his mouth forgot where they were. His mind was fused with a sexually stimulated haze that struck down all focus and sense of time. Even his pursed lips pressed tight couldn't contain what he needed to shout out.

Remembering the baby, Angel placed her hand over his mouth, smiled and rode him harder until she depleted every thing from him that he had to give. He held her while her body calmed, yet her mouth released sensual yelps. He knew she was done when her body fell against his. As she struggled to control her breathing, his hands moved up and down her back. That was his way, without words, of thanking her for allowing him to be free in every way with her.

They stayed like and in the peace of the moment. All he wanted to do was hold her like this forever. There was no more being with a woman and then finding an excuse for getting up and out. There was never any cuddling. There was no lingering around in the moment. In the past, the moment was the act. With Angel, every moment was important. This time warranted giving her his attention; in *every* way.

This was what he meant when he said if he had to give anyone the story of his life at this point, he would say that he gambled on love and he had now won big time. Angel was his prize and he'd never felt luckier.

"When you're ready, I'll take us to bed," he said, wiping the sweat from her forehead, kissing her closed eyelids.

"I want to sit like this for a while. If this is love, I'm glad I finally found it with you. With what you've told me about your past and the way you've blocked yourself off from letting a woman in, I'm glad you gambled on me. I'm glad you are trusting me with your heart and with your love. I promise that I will forever cherish the chance you are taking with me. Being this open and vulnerable with me can't have been an easy step for you."

"Baby?"

"Yes?"

He moved her wet hair out of her face and behind her ears when she leaned up and captured his gaze.

"I want to talk about our future. I know we moved fast to get here. I want to be sure that you know I want you and Marleigh in my life forever. To do that, I need to fix some things with my family. My sisters are going to come for the grand opening party, so you'll get to meet them. I also want my family to meet you and Marleigh. When I say family, I mean my mother too. Of course, you already know about that history. She and my father are why, for so long, I haven't allowed myself to get close to a woman. I didn't want to be like him. In so many ways, I thought I was. I was afraid to love a woman. Now that I am in love, I want nothing more than to open my heart even more. What do you think about that?"

She leaned back and looked into his eyes. He saw tears forming.

"Horace, you are my forever king. I can't wait to meet them all and have them meet Marleigh. We are your family. I wouldn't want it any other way. I couldn't be the woman you love if I didn't encourage you to make things right with your family. Maybe not with your father because I understand your hesitation there. I support you in every way. Tell me what I can do to help you. We are your life. Where you go, we go."

He kissed her sweetly. Everything in him was reminded that falling in love with her was because he was ready. It was the perfect time and place for where his life was taking him.

"After the opening, I'll book us a flight down south. It's time for me to heal. That's the only way that me, you and Marleigh can grow as a family without issues."

"I love you, baby," Angel said.

"Oh? Can I move us to the bed? I want you to show me again."

"I'll race you there!"

Before she could get up and get to the bedroom before him, he stood and placed her over his shoulder. Angel's soft giggles invigorated him. Next up, was loving her for the rest of the night.

"You know, I don't usually go to bed this early," he admitted as he carried her around to turn off the lights and set the alarm.

"We're going to bed? Get Marleigh's monitor off the table," Angel said as she snickered louder when he backtracked to get it.

When they arrived in the bedroom, he placed her in the center.

"Of course we're not going to bed; not really. Not within the next few hours. You just rocked my world by giving me all the feels; I do mean all of them. I'm talking about every single slippery, warm, tight feel."

"That was some good sex. Just damn hot!" Angel declared, reaching for him after she took off the t-shirt and her panties.

She licked her lips when he did the same and stood before her naked and ready to love her again. He moved his own hand up and down the evidence. He sexy grin was all she needed to prepare for a night a loving.

"Yes, it was. We'll sleep another time. This weekend is all about loving, baby – me loving you and you loving me. First, I'm going to run us a hot bath that we can enjoy together. Maybe, just maybe, we can get creative and really work those bubbles up into a frenzy."

"Whew! You cannot threaten me with a good time. I'll get the bubble bath and you bring the monitor."

Horace watched her trot into the bathroom. All he saw was body, body and more body. Nothing brought him more pleasure than to finally know that he'd found his other half. Angel was really his person. They have found each other.

17

Horace walked into the game room on the private level of the casino at the West location. Even though he, along with the men who were sitting around the poker table, should be at work, they were slacking off on a Tuesday morning. Playing hooky from work was Carlos' idea. It had been too long since they had all gotten together and invited him. A few times over the past week or two, he'd gotten the call that they were trying to put a game together. He was otherwise occupied and blew them off. His life was threatened by his best friend, if for any reason, he had declined another poker game.

"Well, look who's dragging in like all is good in the world; as if he hasn't been blowing us off for weeks," Torrence said.

Horace closed the door behind him and grabbed a beer from the beverage center under the long black counter near the door. This was a special room that was only open to a select few people, namely their friends who were here now. He walked around the table and greeted Carter, Dexter, Carlos, Joey and Torrence. He was surprised Tucker wasn't there. He thought Reese's brother, DJ would be here. Perhaps he was running late.

"Don't come for me. Say, where's DJ? I hear I'm not the only one in the group who goes missing," he replied when he got to Torrence. "And, you, of all people, know what my life has been like. I'm here tonight, aren't I?" he asked.

"Only because I threatened you. Angel has you hemmed up like that? As for DJ, the twins have him on lockdown," Torrence said.

"Twins. Here I am at home losing sleep over one baby. Don't get me wrong, I love it. Maia is my world. Two babies at once though?" Joey questioned.

Horace looked around the room and pairs of glaring eyes. He flipped each of them off.

"Oh, please. Don't act like each of you don't know what it's like when you find that woman who makes you want to give her the world because to you, she is your world? Lie if you want, but all of you know what I'm talking about. You all know that we have companies to run? We're gathered, discreetly to play cards in the middle of the day. I take it, this break was needed. I admit, I need the break. All of the executive staff started this week and the new office has been hell. There are tech and phone issues. The desk chairs aren't ergonomic as we thought they were. That means that Rhonda had to request new chairs and return the ones that were recently delivered. Why that wasn't pointed out from the start, I don't know."

Horace stopped complaining and took his seat at the table.

"Ah, the newest member of our crew has bitten the dust. He's been hit by the love bug. Look, I'm not blaming you. I've been around you for months and I get it. There is something about those sisters. I've got one and you have the other. My wife owns all of me. This space, when we're all in it, is a safe space for men. I boldly declare that I would be nothing without my wife. Anybody else feel the same?" Joey asked.

Horace chuckled when every hand in the room went up, including his.

"We warned you about joining our brothers of chi-town crew," Dexter added, taking out the deck of cards.

"Listen, we're not complaining. At least I'm not. I miss seeing and hanging with you outside of the casino. When we gave the staff the weekend off to mentally prepare for the next few months, I just knew we'd connect. I even told that to Reese," Torrence explained and took the deck from Carlos so that he could deal.

"No cigars?" Dexter asked.

"I have some in my duffle bag on the other side of the room," Carter replied and got up to get them.

"I already know you got the good stuff, so bring me two of them," Dexter added.

"I promised Angel some uninterrupted downtime with her and Marleigh. Best weekend ever! That's all I'm going to say about it. The best weekend of my life," Horace expounded.

"Ah, you were knee deep in it?" Dex asked.

"That was a part of the weekend but mostly, it was about talking about where we are as a couple and where we're going. I also wanted to take some time to give her my full attention to talk about what's been going on in her life now that the bad parts are behind her."

"So, she's really done? It's over?" Carter asked.

"It is. Both the criminal and the family court cases are done. She's starting fresh. She's working in the main office at the casino, and loving it. Rhonda loves Angel's eagerness to learn everything and then applying it. She's registered for classes for the upcoming semester. We're talking about taking Marleigh and going to visit my mother and my sisters."

"Hold up. What? Did you just say your mother?" Torrence asked.

Horace hadn't had a chance to talk to fill him in on all that had been going on, especially about his family.

"Yeah, I'll tell you about that. We're not going until weeks after the opening. I want to be here to work through any kinks following the grand opening."

"Kudos for you. Angel is bringing out the greatness in you. That's what a good woman will do for you," Torrence explained.

"Being with her is unlike being with anyone else. You know me and my life in Vegas. I was not a choir boy. I wasn't even invited into the church. Who knew that I would discover wanting a woman forever right here in Chicago?" Horace asked.

He'd been saying that to himself over and over for weeks. He didn't need to convince himself that it was true. He was happy that the moment he knew he wanted her, he didn't let anything stop him.

"I'm telling all of you, there is something in the water here in Chicago. We're under some kind of spell. I fell in love with a woman who almost killed me with a car," Joey said.

"I fell in love with a woman, not just because she had my baby, but because I couldn't begin to imagine my life without her and my son, at that time, sons now," Dexter added.

"Y'all know me and Sienna's story. I actually lost my wife because I was stupid thinking I could do what the joneses were doing. Thank goodness she saw the real me, the good in me and decided to give me a second chance. Having a woman who is ten toes down can mean the difference between misery and happiness," Carter said.

"I'm with you. Everly shattered my life in the past, but when our lives came full circle, I couldn't deny that I wasn't whole without her. Love will do all of this for you and to you. Feel free to miss a lot of poker games if you know your woman needs your devotion with your time. These fools will always be here, except when they are home, laid up with their women like you were this past weekend. I'm just happy that all of drama with that cop is behind her. Can you believe what he tried to pull? He tried to make her lose her kid? He's low," Carlos explained.

Horace heard and knew of all of their stories.

"He is low. Angel's lawyer called her and told her to watch out for this guy. He's done. I wish he would try coming for my woman," Horace professed.

He meant every word. Still, he was keeping an eye out for anyone who appeared to be focused on her when they were out and about. A vengeful ex-cop is a dangerous one. He didn't know what he would do if anyone ever hurt her again.

Horace got up from the table to grab another beer. He was going upstairs for the night after the poker and not to Angel's apartment smelling like smoke and beer. Besides, she had to get up early for work. Her second day had gone smooth. Before he could get back to the game, Torrence walked over to him.

"You're going to do it? You're going to go see your mother?"

Horace nodded. He didn't know what would happen, but it was time he let go of the dead weight he'd been carrying around so that nothing clouds the life he is building with Angel.

"I'm going to do it."

"And your dad?"

"Oh, hell no. He's a clown and not worth a conversation. I'm not interested in a relationship with him. Like he did with me and my brother, he mentally and emotionally abused my sisters. My mother finally woke up and gave him his walking papers. I may be able to repair what is broken between us, but with him, I don't know if I'll ever be ready. Baby steps for the moment."

"Good for you," Torrence said embracing him. "If you feel yourself spiraling down when you visit them, call me day or night and I'll hop on the first plane to pull up."

"I know you will. It's good."

"Say, are you sure Angel isn't in any danger from this Charlie guy?"

"No, she isn't. I can't protect her around the clock but I'm teaching her to watch her surroundings at all times."

"You know Carlos can get her some guys to provide security if you need that. We have to protect our women. Now that you're all in love, does Ace know? I can't imagine she'll take it well hearing a woman finally snagged your heart. Those women in Vegas have been trying to get you to commit for years. Here you are finding your perfect woman in Chicago."

"She is perfect, Torrence. We just work."

"You do look happy. Let's get back to this card game. I don't know about these fools, but my lady is waiting up for me after she puts the baby down. There may be a short window and I plan to be there at the perfect time. Keep Angel close."

"You think he's really going to come for her? I mean, everything is over and done with."

"True, but for him, he's still living through it every day. Just tell her to be careful."

"I got you. Let me take all the money on the table tonight. I'm feeling lucky today," Horace said and retook his seat.

18

Angel couldn't sleep. Even though she needed as much rest as she could get knowing she has a full work day ahead of her, she tossed back and forth across her queen-sized bed. Her legs moved about in a frustrating manner, her legs getting tangled up in the comforter. The uneasy feeling wouldn't go away. Nothing with the girls had her feeling anxious. Both Marleigh and Maia were sleeping soundly in the other bedroom. She'd already checked on them several times. Nothing, by way of any sounds, came across the baby monitor that caused concern. It was an internal feeling. She didn't like it.

Turning on her left side to glance at the clock on her nightstand with large numbers lit up in blue, the time was just after eight in the evening. She and girls were home alone.

After a full day at work, she came home to switch duty with Marlow. She was going to keep the girls tonight. Marlow had decided to go out with a few friends for food and drinks, something she rarely did. Since having Maia, other than a few outings, she preferred staying in. With Joey out with his friends, including Horace, she told Marlow to go out and have fun because she would keep both girls with her all night. The plan was for Marlow and Joey to get home around nine and spend some time alone.

While in the office earlier in the day, she saw Horace for a brief moment when he let her know that after hanging out with his friends, he would stay home since he would already be at the casino. He didn't want to wake any of them up by coming into her apartment late in the evening. He and a group of his friends were planning to spend the day drinking and playing cards. He wasn't planning to go into the office the next day until around noon, while she, on the other hand, enjoyed going in before seven so that she could get home to spend time with Marleigh. Her schedule had only been in place for a while but she missed being with her baby girl. She was getting a second chance at being a mother. She wasn't perfect at it, but she was giving it her all.

When she turned back the other way, she suddenly realized what the problem was. She couldn't roll over and find herself being enclosed in a cocoon that was Horace's arms. They had fallen into a routine where most of the nights during the week, they spent them together. Horace was often so busy that the only times he had, other than Sunday when he worked only when necessary, was late hours, at least for now. He promised her that they would find more quality time after the casino and hotel were open for business. He would be able to turn most of the operations over to his team.

Angel rubbed her hand across the other side of the bed where, if Horace was with her, that is where he would be. She thought about her sister's words. If she feels something for Horace, he was part of a group of men who maintained that when they found the woman of their dreams, they love on her hard and, forever. Horace made sure she knew that she was his forever woman. With them knowing that, they didn't have to work towards anything when it came to their love. It was there for them to enjoy. Still, she missed him. She didn't need him in her bed or her in his every single night to know that they loved each other. It felt good just having his arms around her.

Horace made her feel safe. No other man she'd ever been with had made her feel that way. Not even the men in her family gave her a sense of safety and security. This feeling of being love, adored and cared for was another reason for her to stay on the straight and narrow. She has a good man. She wanted to be everything for him just as he was for her.

A sexy shiver shot through her body when she was reminded of how intensely and passionately he made love to her. Every time he reached for her or she for him, she knew that the greatest pleasure she'd ever experienced was about to happen. She never knew love could be like this. The idea of it brought a smile to her face. When her cell phone vibrated on the nightstand, she grabbed it thinking it was Marlow letting her know that she was on her way home. If so, she would remind her not to come downstairs to get Maia. She would be fine all night.

Instead of the call being from Marlow, it was Horace. She was surprised.

"Baby!" she declared.

"Hi, my love. Did I wake you?"

"No. Even if you did, it would still be okay. There is never a bad time to hear from you. Are you still out with your friends? I assumed it would be a late night."

"It's already been a long day. We've been drinking since noon, though I stopped earlier. Cigars and beer were plentiful thanks to Carter. It was his turn to provide them. The time we're together, I'll bring the sustenance."

"Please tell me you aren't driving? It sounds like you're outdoors. I thought you were going home after?"

"No, babe. I'm not driving. I used one of our private car services for today. I knew I would be drinking and I wasn't sure how late I would be out if the fellas decided to go someplace else after the games ended. I'm actually in the car. I got a call to check something out at the construction site. It wasn't much that needed my attention. I guess the guys just wanted to be sure I was in the loop. When I got back in the car, I thought about you. I'm always thinking about you. I was wondering what sexy little number you had on tonight for bed. Or, are those barely-there nighties just for me?"

"I keep those strictly for you. I do have on a short, satin nightie. It's a warm night. I miss you. I was awake when you called because I was missing having you beside me."

"I know how you feel. You need to get up early which is why I'm going home. Besides, I smell like smoke and alcohol."

"I love all of your smells."

"Angel, this is not my usual smell, sweetheart. I can't wait to get a shower when I get in."

"Ohhh, I love you all wet and slick."

"Mmm, I love you the same way, especially the slippery part. How are the girls doing? I know you didn't let them go to sleep this early. Marlow is going to kill you. Didn't you tell me that she asks you to keep them up as late as possible so that they will sleep all night?"

"She did, but they were sleepy. After I fed them, I tried playing with them to keep them awake. They got fussy and tired of me. I gave them baths and they both fell asleep in the middle of me putting on their pajamas. I'm okay if they get up in the middle of the night. They're staying down here with me.

Marlow said she'll come down in the morning with them when I leave for work if they are still asleep."

"How was work today?"

"Busy. I had the assignment of going through the list of special guests for the grand opening festivities. I didn't realize there is almost a week-long list of events before you actually open the casino. I was star-struck all day. It was great. You sound so tired. You should have let the casino issue resolve itself in the morning."

"I wanted to tire out the alcohol in my system. You know I hate going to bed until I'm more lucid."

Angel knew that about him. She remembered one night when he spent the night with her after going out for drinks with a client. It was in the middle of the night, on a weekend. He was going to go home. She really wanted to see him. Not caring about the time, she told him to come to her. She may be asleep, but she would love to wake up in his arms. The fact that he felt the same way was why he didn't protest. He was more concerned about waking her and Marleigh up by coming through so late. His plan to not wake her up didn't play out that way. She heard him stumbling around in the dark trying to be quiet. Once he made it to the shower, temptation took over. She slipped out of bed, removing one of his t-shirts that she loved sleeping in and joined him in the shower. She learned a wonderful lesson; drunk shower sex is the best. He let her do all kinds of freaky things. When they finally made it to bed, he slept like a baby. In the morning, she and Marleigh left him sleeping and watched television until he woke. Though a little hungover and with a slight headache from the night before, Horace still made them breakfast. and she made them breakfast.

"I know. Are you okay?" she questioned. There was still something about his voice.

"Yeah. Well, sort of."

"Horace?"

"Okay. Though Carter and Dex were going out and everyone else was going home to their families, I found myself jealous that I was going home to an empty space. I have an early morning meeting at the original hotel, so I should go home."

"You don't have to. You know that, right? You make a point of always being where I need you to be when I need you to. I am here, baby."

"I know. I'm going to delay my arrival in the morning. You need sleep. Did I forget to mention that I ordered lunch for everyone in the office tomorrow? I don't know why that came up just now."

"Did you? That's wonderful. I have the kindest, most wonderful man."

"I meant to tell Rhonda about the delivery. Can you let her know in the morning? It's a large spread. She can have them set up in one of the conference rooms, probably the large one. It's a lot of food. Will I see you tomorrow after work? I have kind of a late day. I won't smell like cigars."

"You can see me anytime you want. I'll be here at home after work. I'm going to do some online shopping for some stuff for Marleigh. I was planning on relaxing. Do you want to come by after you get off?"

"I do. I want to see you right now. I'm not far from you. Am I asking too much if I come by for a hug and kiss? I don't want to stay. I just want to see you. I sleep better when we're together. Tonight, a kiss will work just fine."

"Yes. I'm up. A hug and kiss may be what I need to get to sleep."

"You won't mind the smell?"

"I already told you that I love all of your smells."

"Twenty minutes?"

Angel was already up and out of her bed. She turned on the big light. She started looking through her things to slip on a pair of shorts and a t-shirt. Then she looked down at herself and her slinky nightie and decided to leave it on. She wouldn't mind him copping a feel or two for good measure.

She sniggered to herself at the thought of his sexy gropes of all of her curves.

"Yes. I'll be here. You know the code or use your key if you have it with you. "

"I have it."

"I love you. I'll see you in a few then."

"Yes, baby. Yes, you will."

In anticipation after the call ended, Angel danced around the room like she was at a concert. Seeing him would definitely put the icing on her cake that is this day. She would then be ready for bed.

**

Charlie took out his stock of white powdery substance and indulged again. The night was still early. He had hoped that Angel would venture out someplace alone so that he could make her pay for ruining his life. Here he was thinking she was living on skid row when all along, she was living the high-life off of her rich brother-in-law.

"How can someone as low-life as you be related to Joey Dreads? Where was he when you could barely afford to feed you and your baby?" he said to himself.

If anyone could see him sitting inside of his car, both drunk and now high, they would think he was living on that same skid row street where Angel had been living. He had fallen; not just a little, but *way* down. He still didn't know who he was after all that had happened to him. He couldn't get himself together. No doubt, he wouldn't until Angel was no longer a vision in his nightmares. Other women had tried, but none had ever taken him down like her. How pathetic was he?

Charlie looked through the front window of his car at her house at the end of the block on the opposite side of the street. He'd been sitting here about an hour, unable to start the car and leave. Stalking had become the name of the game.

After seeing her strolling down the street the other day as if she didn't have a care in the world, he had to come back. He had to get her. There would be a day when she came out of her house alone. That's when he would make his move.

The need to use the restroom took over. It was time to drive off. His obsession with her would have him coming back to fight another day. He would keep coming back until his luck paid off.

Just as he was about to put his car in park, a black SUV pulled up to Angel's house. It stopped in the middle of the street. Being curious, he left the car in park and waited. Seconds later, the man, he now knows as Angel's boyfriend, some casino owner, exited the back passenger side of the car. After saying something to the driver, he walked over to the house and went inside.

"Probably coming over for a booty call. What a nice booty she has."

He had seen it for himself and dreamed about seeing it in the flesh.

Charlie was angry knowing that it was supposed to be him hitting Angel off. She appears to like to share herself with men, but just not him. At least if his life was going to be ruined by her, he could have gotten what he wanted from her first.

The car that her boyfriend had gotten out of pulled off and ended up on the corner opposite him. It was apparent that Loverboy wasn't going to be staying all night. He wanted to get a closer look at him. He decided to wait. Maybe he was picking Angel up. It wasn't too late. He could see where they liked to go. He couldn't believe how lucky she was; rich brother-in-law, rich boyfriend.

He tried to catch a glimpse of the driver of the truck. He couldn't see in. He also knew that the same man couldn't see him either. He sat and waited. He looked like any other person sitting in a car. There was nothing odd about his presence. It would be if anyone knew who he was.

Not five minutes later, Horace, whom he was able to get a lot of information on, came out of the house and looked around for the truck. The moment he saw it, Charlie acted on instinct and not on common sense. Alcohol and drugs were driving his actions.

He started the car up and shifted it into drive just as Horace was taking his time walking across the street. He wasn't in a rush. It was more of a stroll. His smile of happiness angered Charlie. He hated the man and didn't even know him.

Without thinking, Charlie sped up and just Horace had made it to the middle of the street, he made a sharp left turn. Before he could stop himself, when at the last minute, he tried to swerve to not hit him, he did hit him and Horace's body landed on the hood of the car. Not knowing what to do, in a panic, Charlie sped off but didn't get far. He swerved to the left and the body fell off of the car into the street. Charlie lost control of the wheel and rammed into an oncoming car. His head hit the steering wheel and that was all he remembered; that and the massive ringing in his head. His last thought was that he'd just done something else stupid. That was it. He was done and he was out.

19

"Horace! Horace! Where are you? Horace!"

Angel screamed out his name as she raced down the hall of the hospital where he'd been taken after being hit by a car. Her legs wobbled. Her head turned from left to right as she looked for anyone who would help her find him. In her chest, her heart felt like it was going to explode. She was out of it, yelling and looking in every direction for any sight of him. Her world was spinning out of control. The love of her life was somewhere in the building. The one man who showed her a new and different side of life filled with love, understanding and unconditional faith in who she wanted to be now that she had turned her life around. As far as she knew, he could have been taken from her.

Angel dared to think that. She wiped that thought from her mind immediately. Horace would want her to think positive. She stopped moving and immediately sent him love and happy vibes. He had to make it; not just for her and Marleigh, but for everyone he impacted.

She couldn't catch her breath. Angel huffed in frustration as her hair annoyingly fell across her face. It was in the way. Her hair wasn't important but the tendrils continuing to cover her eyes made getting her hair out of the way a priority. She needed to concentrate on Horace and what had happened. In a blink of an eye, he went from smiling and waving to being spread out on the ground at her feet.

All she remembered was him stopping at her house before going home. They talked only for a few minutes. They wanted to lay their eyes on each other to make their day happily complete.

With only a few minutes together, Horace had kissed her senseless. She walked him out to the steps where after a last kiss good night and hearing his sensual, *'I love you'*, he walked off in search of his driver. She stood at the top of the steps that led to the apartment, still with the baby monitor in her hand. When he turned to wave at her after stepping off of the curb, a scene out of a horror movie played out. A car coming right at him struck him at waist level. She watched in dismay as Horace rolled over onto the top of the car, his body flailing like a rag doll. When the driver tried to pull away with Horace on the car, she watched in fear as his body rolled off and hit the street with a thud that she could easily hear. She stomped in place out of fear that he could have been seriously hurt and she couldn't get to him.

Seconds later, the car hit another car. That crash was heard by a plethora of people who rushed over to see what happened. She didn't know what to do. The girls were in the house and she couldn't leave them. All she could do was scream for someone to call an ambulance.

Angel started to race back into the house when Marlow pulled up in her car. Before she turned into the garage on the other end of their end-of-group brownstone, Angel screamed for her which stopped her sister from driving further. Marlow looked toward the commotion happening on the street. When she turned her head back to her, Angel cried and yelled Horace's name.

Vibing like only she could with her sister, Marlow knew. She hopped out of the running car and raced over to her. The only words she could get out were that the girls were sleeping and Horace had been hit by a car. Marlow told her to run to Horace and she would check on the girls while calling 911. Angel then took off running. Everything after that was a blur.

Somehow, she'd made it to the hospital in the truck that Horace had arrived to her house in. His driver saw what happened and couldn't do a thing. Once the ambulance and police arrived minutes later, it was then that she could see who was in the car that had hit him. It was Charlie.

She discovered that was the case as she tried to talk to Horace, who was delirious. Convincing him to lie still was a task when he kept trying to get up. It was clear he didn't understand what had happened to him.

The police arrived and raced up to her and Horace. She tried to calm herself long enough to tell them what happened. When the tears wouldn't stop falling, she had to keep wiping them away to be able to see through her blocked vision. Her man was hurt and lying in the street. What troubled her the most was that she couldn't tell how badly he was injured. That's why she continued to beg him to be still because help was coming.

She ended up sitting on the ground next to Horace until the ambulance loaded him up and sped off. Left standing and unsure of what to do, Marlow yelled at her and pointed to the driver of Horace's truck. She yelled that she'd reached Joey and Torrence, who called the driver. They gave him an instruction was to get her to the hospital.

Angel looked down at herself and she was still in her night clothes. Running to the house on pure adrenalin, she raced inside, crying uncontrollably and trying to explain to Marlow that it was Charlie who hit him. Marlow helped her get dressed and pushed her out the door letting her know that she would remain with the girls.

When she turned and raced back out of the house with her phone in her hand and dressed in sweat pants and a t-shirt, she rushed to the truck and hopped in. Horace's driver took off, driving like he was in the *Fast & Furious* movie series.

Once at the hospital, she didn't see where they had taken Horace. All she could do was call his name. When two security guards raced up to her to stop her from going further into the emergency room, she tried to push her way through them.

"Let her go!"

A familiar voice from behind her got everyone's attention in the hall. It was Joey. The guards didn't let go of her arm. They continued to struggle with her saying she couldn't go back.

"He said, let her go!" Torrence forcibly yelled.

Joey stepped up and pushed the guards back, taking his place between her and them.

The guys started to test Joey's stance and then they recognized him. Both threw their hands up in surrender.

"You're Joey Dreads," one of the guards said.

"I know who I am. With that out in the open, I said don't touch her. You know who I am. Therefore, I suggest you get someone in charge and step back. Touch her again and I'll happily go to jail. That is, after I'm done with both of you. I won't be nice about it again."

Angel turned to Torrence and held onto him.

"Torrence, where is he? Where did they take him?" she cried.

The guards apologized and moved out of the way. Others in the hall were focused on Joey. Just then a nurse walked up and spoke directly to him. There wasn't a person, especially women, who did not recognize Joey and his long dreadlocks. He was just as famous for his looks as he was for his presence in the wrestling ring.

"Come with me," a nurse said to her and Joey. Torrence followed them.

"Where is he?" she asked again.

"You're here for Horace Grant, right"

A police officer appeared from out of nowhere and stepped between them and the nurse. Angel and Joey ignored the cop and focused on the nurse who had stopped walking to explain.

"We were called by the ambulance when he was in route here," she said.

"Is it bad?" Angel asked.

"He's currently being looked at by our on-call emergency room team. I don't have any other information for you at this time other than to say he's awake and alert."

Before she could say anything else, another officer walked up to Joey and introduced himself.

"Déjà vu," Joey said.

"You remember me?" the cop asked.

"I do. You were the one my family and I spoke with after my accident well over a year ago," Joey said. "I never forget a face," he added.

"I am. I was here on another case when I saw you race in and thought I'd check to see what's going on."

The first cop spoke up again.

"Are you the family of Horace Grant?" he asked.

"I am," Angel said.

"Oh? You are?"

Angel looked to Torrence and Joey. She had to get information on how he was doing. She wasn't his family, but right now, no one was closer. Joey spoke up for her.

"She is his wife. This is Angel. This right here is his best friend, Torrence. We're family because I'm married to her sister. It's a lot, but anything you can tell us would be great," Joey said.

The cop tried to move them to the side, but Angel refused to go. She wanted to see Horace.

"I promise, as soon as you can go back or if I get any information on how he's doing, I'll come right out to get you," the nurse explained.

Angel nodded and took Joey's hand. Together, they turned to the cops.

"Okay, I'm not really supposed to tell you all of this, but here is what I know. I was a block away when I heard the crash. I raced over and Mr. Grant was on the ground. He was conscious and not lucid enough to answer any questions. From what others at the scene were able to tell us, the car went right for him. The driver is..."

Angel cut him off.

"He's an ex-cop named Charlie. There is history there. I thought I saw him a few times, but didn't believe my eyes. I brushed it off. He's been following me for a while. I just didn't know. He hit Horace on purpose. I saw it all. He came right at him. He never even hit the break. This is all my fault," she cried.

"Whoa, none of this is your fault," Joey offered.

"Yes, it is. I brought him into our lives."

"Don't carry that around," Torrence added. "This was that guy's fault; plain and simple. Horace and I were talking about him just a few hours ago. We were wondering if he was dangerous. We now have our answer," Torrence said.

"Well, he was detained. He was looked at on the scene and his injuries were minor because of the air bag. He's been taken to the station. You won't have to worry about him. He's being booked right now. I don't have the information on the charges yet, but I will reach out. Can I get contact information from someone?" the cop asked.

"Use mine," Joey said.

"Mr. Kincaid, come with me over to this corner so that I can get your information. Miss, I'm sorry this has happened. I hope your husband will be okay."

"He had better be or Charlie will wish he'd been more injured!" she yelled. Now that anger replaced fear, Angel's teared stopped. She began focusing on being the woman Horace needs her to be right now. He needs her thinking and doing any and everything he needs.

"I think he's going to be fine," Torrence said.

"Can you call his sisters and his mother? I know he's been in contact with them. Here is Horace's phone. I got it off of him at the scene. I knew I would need it," she said.

"I have their numbers. Horace gave them to me in case of a serious emergency. I will call them as soon as we get an update on his injuries," Torrence noted.

Angel nodded and paced. She needed to hear something about the man she loved. Her mind raced with thoughts of always going with her feelings. She had been on edge lately.

She thought she was being followed a few times. She shook it off and didn't focus like Horace had told her to do. How could she not realize that her sixth sense was telling her that Charlie had been around? She thought she'd spotted him a few times over the past few weeks.

Finding a seat, Angel sat and tried to calm her nerves. Torrence and Joey each tried to keep her calm. After what seemed like forever, she heard her name being called. When she looked up, Marlow came running down the hall followed by their mother. They were together? Her mind was now playing tricks on her. Marlow raced over and pulled her into a tight hug. Her mother then pulled both of them into a group hug.

"How is he?" Marlow asked.

"Where are Marleigh and Maia?" Angel asked. She didn't see either baby with her.

"Steven is watching them. They were still asleep when we left," Marlow explained. "He's their godfather. They're good."

"Don't worry about the girls. He'll look after them until one or both you get home," Delores said.

"I'm not leaving until Horace does," Angel shared without a thought.

"I know, sis. I got you. Remember that I am always here for whatever you need. Marleigh is good; she's safe. You focus on Horace and I'll focus on her," Marlow offered.

"Thank you. We haven't heard anything on Horace so far. Everything happened so fast. I saw him Marlow. *Charlie.* I saw him earlier but then I thought that couldn't be possible. It was him. It was him," Angel said.

"Charlie did this?"

"Yes, he did."

"That cop who tried to ruin your life but instead had his torn down like a house of cards?" Marlow asked.

"Yes. What if Horace was seriously hurt because of me? I will never forgive myself," Angel bemoaned.

"Stop it. You are not to blame for this. Keep happy, healthy thoughts. That is what will get him through," Delores said.

Angel nodded and sat back down next to Marlow. She smiled when her sister held her hand and gave it a reassuring squeeze.

"Do you need me to go home with the girls?" Joey asked Marlow.

He walked over and kissed Marlow on the lips.

"No, babe. My brother has this. You're needed here. I was sitting in this exact same spot the day of your accident. Do you remember this is where you were?" Marlow asked him.

"I do. The cop right there is the same one that spoke to my family after the accident. Talk about crashing into love," he replied and winked at her.

"I remember him. He talked to me that night as well. It's crazy that we are here again," Marlow declared.

"I know. Just like before with me, Horace will be okay too. Like your mother said, good, happy and healthy thoughts."

"Mrs. Grant?"

Everyone looked up and then over at Angel when he spoke. She knew they were wondering who they were calling Mrs. Grant as if she were married to Horace. Angel knew she would need to address that with her sister and mother later; just not right now. She stood and put a pin in addressing that later.

"How is he?" she asked.

"He's going to be fine. He's got some serious bumps and bruises but nothing is broken. He's in great shape. The brunt of the force was to his side. He said he tried to hold onto the car and then in a split second made sure he was up on it and not on the ground under it. He's asking for you. You're Angel, right?" the doctor asked.

"Yes."

"Great. We're going to keep him for one night. He has some deep cuts that will require stitches. Overall, he's a very lucky man. Only one of you can go in to see him," the doctor explained.

"That's me," Angel spoke up and walked toward the hospital double doors before anyone could say anything.

"He's in room two-thirty-two at the end of the hall. You can go in until we have a room for him on a floor. We're working on that now. He's a lucky man. That could have been so much worse if his brain hadn't told him how to react to keep from breaking anything or worse."

"Thanks for all that you're doing."

Without additional words, Angel raced to the end of the hall, slid the glass door open and there Horace was. He was lying still in bed with his head turned to the side, his eyes closed. She started crying softly. Walking over to the side of the bed, she caressed his face to let him know that she was there. Looking him over, Angel saw scratches on the left side of his face. There was a clear fluid covering them that the nurse probably put on to keep them from getting infected. She wouldn't touch them with her hand. Instead, she leaned over and kissed him on the lips. That got his attention.

"Mmm, you're here. They told me my wife was out there screaming for me," he chuckled.

When he grimaced from the pain, she took his hand in hers.

"No laughing. I heard that you don't have anything broken but you're bruised up pretty bad. I'm sure it will be painful to laugh. You scared me. I was so scared. I'm so sorry. It was Charlie. Can you believe it? I was supposed to be watching out for him. If I had followed my instincts, I would have said I have been seeing him in the neighborhood. My mind didn't register it was him. I'm so sorry, Horace."

"Baby."

"What?"

"No. You hardly ever call me by my name. It's usually either baby or babe. A few times it was honey. I especially love when you call me, boo. When did you decide to go back to calling me, Horace? Who am I to you?"

His eyes widened as he waited for her to understand.

What he was trying to say didn't register. When it did, instead of crying, she laughed. A few seconds later, she began to cry again.

"You're my baby, my babe, the man I love more than life itself."

"Come here," Horace said, trying to move over on the bed to make room for her.

"I don't think I'm supposed to do that."

"Who says," Horace strained to say and move. "I need you close."

"Baby," she said.

When he smiled and winked at her, she smiled too. She'd just made him happy.

"Up here," he said, patting the side of the hospital bed.

Angel looked around for a seat and then decided, if what he wanted was for her to be on the bed with him, that's what she would do. Making sure to take up as little room as possible, she climbed up and watched Horace's face for any sign that all of her movements were hurting him. She could tell he was holding back letting her see his pain.

"Are you okay?"

"I'm perfect now that you're here next to me. Where's the baby?"

"At the house with my brother. Marlow, my mother, Joey and Torrence are in the waiting area."

"Okay. I didn't see her with you. That's my girl."

"Yes, she is. How are you feeling?"

"Like I've been hit by a car."

"Did anyone tell you?"

"About Charlie? Yes. Before the ambulance took off, a cop asked me if I knew him. I didn't say much, but I told them yes."

"I told them there is history there."

"Look, it will all be sorted out. As much as I know that you may want to talk about this, I don't. I want to lay here and be thankful that I am here with my baby right here in bed next to me. He will be dealt with. If we thought he was done before, he is really done now. I want to leave that for another day. This could have been worse, but it wasn't. Kiss me," he whispered next to her face when he slowly turned in her direction.

Angel didn't hesitate. She was ecstatic that he was able to ask her for a kiss and he was here for her to give him one.

Turning, she held his face and kissed him soft at first, not sure if there was pain. His handsome face was scratched but not scarred.

When she tried to pull away, Horace pulled her back in and this time, showed her what he meant by kissing him.

"The only thing that's been on my mind is you. Just for a second, I realized I could have left this world and left you and Marleigh. That alone had me fighting to stay here. My life with the two of you is everything."

"You're our world, too," Angel answered before her words were cut off by another breath-stealing kiss.

He moaned against her lips. Where he would usually have his hands everywhere when they kissed, she took control, caressing his jaw before plundering his mouth with one grateful kiss after another. Her eyes gazed into his and found them heavy-lidded with desire. She exhaled and smile gallantly.

"Even now, that's what you're thinking about?" she spoke breathlessly against his lips.

"What? I can't help it if any interaction with my woman gets a rise out of me. You should shift your hand down a bit and you'll see what I'm talking about," he laughed.

"You are relentless. Not here – or at least, not now."

"Okay, y'all are nasty. Cut it out! Y'all better not be trying to get into any freaky in this hospital. The cops will be here for a different reason. You'll be home soon enough with her. Keep it in your pants." Torrence said interrupting them. "That goes for you too, Angel. No dipping with the hands," he added, shaking his head at them.

Angel bellowed over in laughter after being caught. Horace tried to join her but yelped in pain all with a smile on his face.

"Either get out or get use to me devouring my woman at any time and in any place. That fool tried to kill me tonight and take me away from her. I'm never letting her go. After all, I understand she's going by Mrs. Grant these days," Horace clapped back.

Angel put her head on his chest and laughed more. To say that she was happy just to be able to hold him like this couldn't begin to describe her joy. She couldn't wait until they, along with Marleigh, are relaxing at home again; together.

"I'm seeing it as a prelude to some kind of reality," Torrence said.

"Man, you already know. That's why we're best friends. You can see where my mind is. No way will I walk through this life without my woman forever," Horace said, kissing her forehead.

Angel laid still and held him tight.

"You good?" Torrence asked him.

"I'm going to be."

"We'll talk about this later?" Torrence questioned.

Angel looked up at Horace and waited for his response.

"That we will. Right now, I just want to lay here with my baby and realize how this could have been a different outcome."

"I need to get your vitals, Mr. Grant," a nurse said, coming up behind Torrence.

"I just stopped in to check on you. I can't stay anyway. They say only one person in here with you at a time. I'll tell the others to forget coming back. The scene in front of me is perfect. It's all love. And if anyone thinks that Angel will trade places with them right now for a visit with you, they are sadly mistaken. I wouldn't change this picture perfect scene for anything; not even to let our friends in."

"Tell them to give me a little more time with him. I promise they will each get to come back and say hello. I need to lay with him like this for now," Angel answered.

"I already know that too. That makes me happy. Seeing him with someone is exactly what a big brother would want; even if it's by relationship and not by blood. Either of you can call me day or night, at any hour, if you need anything. I'll go give your sisters and your mother a call to let them know what happened. I wanted to wait until I knew for sure what your status was. I'm happy to know that I still have my brother for life."

"You can't put and keep a good brother like me down. I'm always going to rise, especially to be sure I'm always around for my two girls. The casino," Horace said.

"Do I need to leave?" Angel asked the nurse.

When the nurse looked to her and then to Horace, she had her answer and snuggled closer.

"You can stay. I'll need his other arm."

"Don't you be in here worried about the casino. I have it all covered. Your only job is to get better and go home with your woman and hug on your little girl. If I see you anywhere near the casino over the next seven days, I'll have security throw you out. You know how Carlos is about instructions. Mine will be that no one is to let you in. Angel, talk to your husband," Torrence chuckled.

"He's not going anywhere but here for now. After this, it's home with me."

"Good. I'll call Rhonda to let her know you'll need at least this week off. The team will be okay while you're out. Horace is the priority. Remember, anything you need, I'm here. I'll be back tomorrow morning to check on you on my way to work. My cell will be on all night."

Torrence waved at them and left.

When the nurse was finished with Horace, Angel snuggled closer.

"I don't know what I would have done without you. I was so scared."

Horace pulled her closer.

"Baby, I'm here. I'm not going anywhere unless it's home with you, just like you said. I know it was scary. It was for me too. Reality is you're here with me, in your favorite place; my arms. We're good. I'm still out here gambling at love and winning at life as long as I have my baby by my side," Horace replied.

Angel nodded as his voice began to fade. Now that she knew he was fine, she was exhausted. Like he said, she was in her favorite place. She smiled and fell asleep.

20

Horace tried his best not to move around too much. He wasn't in as much pain as he had been a week ago after being discharged from the hospital. His bruises were healing and the scratches and cuts were barely noticeable even with the bandages off. Being laid up for a week was starting to get to him. He guessed that happens when you have a woman who refuses to let you lift a finger. Angel had truly been his real angel since being released.

Grabbing the remote to the television, he changed the channel to catch up on his favorite S.W.A.T. episodes. Hondo was the man keeping people safe in one of his favorite places in the country, Los Angeles. He made sure the volume was turned all the way down as to not wake up Marleigh who was sprawled across his chest, sound asleep. He loved the sound of her tiny snores. He leaned down and kissed her forehead, making sure she was comfortable.

"Let me put her in her crib," Angel said walking into the bedroom with a tray with fresh fruit, soup and his favorite, a grilled cheese sandwich with honey ham in the middle.

For a week, he'd been staying with her at the apartment so that she could look after him, especially after she got in from work. She'd stayed home two days before he told her he would be fine just relaxing while she was at work. He tried going home, but Angel wouldn't hear of it. It was either she and Marleigh stayed with him at the casino apartment or he would be staying with them. Knowing that Marlow would sometimes need Angel to help her with Maia since Joey was out of town on business travel with his brother, Horace opted to stay with her. All of their friends made sure that one or some of them stopped by every day with meals or just to keep him company. He agreed to stay with her until he returned to work in a few days. For now, he'd been conducting work virtually. Thankfully, Torrence and his team were handling everything.

During the day, Marlow still had both girls. After a few days, they all learned that in order for Marleigh to not kick up a fuss, he had to remain quiet and in the apartment. If she got one sighting or whiff of him, she wanted him and would cry until the heavens came down if Marlow didn't hand her over to him. Finally, they resorted to letting Marleigh stay with him for most of the day.

"I want to hold her a little longer. I'm still reeling from the idea that the accident could have been worse. I may not have been able to hold her like this ever again. Before you got home from work, Marlow tried to take her upstairs. Guess what?" he questioned.

"I'm listening," Angel said, putting away the laundry that he'd done while she was out.

"She called me Dada."

Angel stopped in her tracks. Horace knew that would get her undivided attention.

"What? She said that?"

"I swear. Ask your sister. I was sitting out in the living room and Marleigh was in her playpen. Marlow picked her up to give her lunch. When Marlow tried to take her upstairs and she figured out she wouldn't be down here with me, she screamed Dada over and over and reached her arms out to me. She fell out in Marlow's arms, screaming like she was being kidnapped. Marlow brought her back down. I told her to bring me her lunch and I would feed her. The minute she was back in my arms, she looked over at Marlow and laughed like she'd just won the lottery. Your sister just shook her head."

"She really called you that?"

"Yes, and it was music to my ears. I started to get emotional but didn't want her to think I was sad. Does that bother you? I know I'm not her father."

"Babe, you're the only father she knows. Joey is a father figure, but you've been in the role of father since we first met. If it doesn't bother you, it certainly doesn't bother me."

Angel went around to the other side of the bed and snuggled up with him and Marleigh.

"I'm not bothered. I'm actually encouraged."

"Oh?" she asked him.

Angel actually sounded surprised. Why, he wasn't sure.

"Stay here and don't move," Horace said getting up slowly with Marleigh in his arms. He was taking great care to not wake her up. He left the bedroom and took her to her room, easily laying her in her crib, before he left out, he placed her gray elephant next to her. He waited a few seconds to be sure she wouldn't wake up. Before leaving, he placed a quick kiss on his finger tips and then transferred the kiss to her cheek.

Going back into the bedroom, he ignored the food and climbed in bed next to Angel.

"You are watching S.W.A.T, again?" she questioned before turning the volume up a little.

"You already know. It's my favorite series."

He turned to face her, taking the remote from her hands. "You're moving a lot better."

"I have an appointment with my doctor tomorrow. I'm expecting the all clear to return to work. With the exception of a slight limp, which he says will eventually clear up with rehab and exercise, I'm all good. Going back to work won't hurt anything. The opening is coming up. I need to get back in the office."

"It's not too soon?" Angel asked.

"No. It's not too soon for a lot of things."

Showing her before telling her, he reached over and pulled her onto his lap.

"Babe, it may be too soon for that," she explained even as he pulled her tankini up and over her head, leaving her naked from the waist up.

Hearing her protest about his bruises, or whatever she was saying, he leaned forward and made a circle around one nipple and then the other with his tongue. If nothing else silenced her so that she could join the moment, he knew this would.

"There is no such thing. It's been over a week. A brother is tortured every time you walk by. I promise, it's not too soon. We have a small window with Marleigh out like a light for about another hour. Marlow and Maia are out, which means we're alone. Lift up."

Even while she still tried to convince him that sex right now was too soon, when she lifted her body up so that he could take her shorts and panties off, she knew how much he needed her and gave in. They had been abstaining from this kind of sex since he came home. They did other sexy things. There were no limits to their love and intimacy. More than anything else, he missed being inside of her. That was the closeness he needed right now.

When she lowered her body back to his lap, he accepted the heated kiss that she planted on him.

"Are you sure," Angel spoke against his lips before he captured hers in an intense kiss that showed just how much he'd missed all of her. A soft, needy moan escaped her lips.

Just like that, the kiss turned ravaging. The idyllic bliss that Horace was experiencing, he wanted to last forever. His arms closed around her back. Angel leaned more into him and their salacious kissing exchange.

Angel's hand reached between them until her hands pulled out what she was in search of. She rose her hips again. This time, it was to slide his sweat pants and boxers down low enough that she could get both of her hands around his straining flesh. Her hands stroked him as he suckled her breast into his mouth. He throbbed relentlessly in her hands. Her touch sent surges of amatory electricity through his body. His hips pulsed as her hands moved salaciously faster. He leaned up and the hazy look in her eyes told him that she was as ready as he was. The moisture on his sweat pants was another sign.

He reached between them and slid one and then two fingers inside of her body now slick with her natural moisture.

"I need to be inside of you, baby. Right now."

Proving his point, Horace shifted her around on his lap. He positioned her right where they both needed him to be.

"Yes," she expressed against his neck along a vein he could feel straining with penetrating need.

Horace lifted her and easily slid inside where her silky walls seduced him before they began moving. When Angel leaned back, placing her hands on his thighs, she started to lift until only the tip of him was left inside of her. She teasingly slid back down.

Horace held to her hips and guided her, setting a faster pace. He leaned his body forward and flicked his tongue over and over against her lips, tempting her provocatively until her hips rushed up and down faster without his assistance.

He grasped her hips tighter in his hands.

"I think this is going to be quick baby. You feel so delicious. I'm trying to hold back, but you're pulling everything out of me that I thought I'd have better control over."

His erection throbbed. His legs began to tremble under her fixated gyrations.

"I'm with you, baby. I'm there."

With her hands braced on the top of the headboard behind his head, her body slammed down on his. She writhed wildly over him. Making sure she shared an amazing orgasm with him, he slipped one hand between them and over her sexy womanly folds. Sliding fingers across her straining, pulsing titillating nub, he held her as she screamed through her release. Her body enjoying a sizzling orgasm ended up triggering his own orgasmic euphoria. He roared under his breath. His hips pumped wildly. His body rode out the sheer magnitude of completion that he'd been craving for a week. He closed his eyes against the bright lights blasting off in his head in the same manner of blasts his body was going through.

Realizing Angel's reaction to their lovemaking, he knew that if he didn't do something, her screams would wake the baby.

He gathered her lips and suckled the screams of passion from her mouth and into his. He smiled against her lips, remembering the number of times she did the same for him when he wanted to howl at the moon. Their tongues sought out and loved each other hard in a desperate need to speak their pleasure without words.

Riding out the storm of the unmeasurable climax that slammed into him again and again, Horace had to hold tighter to Angel to keep her from falling from his lap. He gave to her until she had collected every essence of the erotic moment that she needed.

He loved all of her. He wanted all of her. Not just tonight, but forever. Nothing like the chemistry they shared has ever graced his life before. No one made him desire a life beyond now before her. He needed forever. Perhaps this wasn't the right time, but they were perfectly in sync in every way.

Horace waited until the ability to speak was formed in his mouth. He held Angel's face in the palm of both of his hands. Kissing her again and again, he was overwhelmed by the depth of his love for all of her following yet another perfect coital entanglement. He stopped kissing her. Neither of them moved. They sat like that, his hands caressing her face while her hands shifted from the headboard to his shoulders.

"I love you so much! You have been more than I feel I deserve. I don't know when this kind of love developed but it's in every part of me; my mind, my body, my spirt, my heart, my love. It's all you. It's nobody but you. I'm not talking about just now. I mean forever. I could have lost you. I know I was the one hit by the car. Something tells me that it was meant for you. We may never know, but that's what I've been feeling. I think he meant to take you away from me for good. The opportunity to hurt me knowing it would kill you if anything happened to me is what he counted on. Our love had another plan. A forever plan. I don't believe in following anyone else's fads or trends. What my friends say happened to them when they met their women, I can say has happened to me. I also want to believe that meeting you and Marleigh and loving you both like the family I've always wanted to have, was meant to be. Can you see me and you like this forever? I sure can. I want that," he avowed. "I love you with all of me."

Angel nodded and cried. Horace kissed her tears away.

"I could have lost you that day. When I saw you lying on the ground, I prayed that all that I had done in life that wasn't good wasn't sending Karma my way. You didn't deserve that. Neither did I. I did, however deserve you. I want us forever. You made me see that I am worthy of real, true love. I feel so beautiful, sexy and desirable all the time. You push me and encourage me every day. We are a team. There isn't a better team anywhere. I love you like crazy. I'm just glad that we are getting this chance to continue what we started months ago."

"Baby, I shudder to think of what could have been a totally different outcome. I think if I don't do what's in my heart, I would be slapping this thing called life in the face. I don't have what I want right now or need for what I'm about to do, but by the time the sun goes down tomorrow, I will," he declared, kissing her again.

"Horace, baby, whatever it is, as long as we get to stay like this, I'm down for whatever."

He smiled and winked, a usual exchange from him to her.

"Are you down for marrying me and making me, you and Marleigh a real family? I'm talking the kind of family that nothing and no one could ever take from us. I want to marry

199

you. I want to adopt her and give you both my last name. One day, when we're ready, I want to have babies with you that will have our combined looks, but mainly your gorgeousness. I love you. Would you agree to be my wife and love me forever?"

Horace waited, but not long.

"I would marry you right now if a justice of the peace was standing right here."

"Well, maybe not right here, right now. That would be embarrassing considering I am still buried deep, deep inside of you, but I get the point. You're saying yes, baby."

"Yes. I am saying yes now, forever and always."

"Folks at the hospital were already calling you Mrs. Grant."

"I loved every time they did. That gave me hope. I took it as a sign that one day, I wasn't sure when, that would be my reality."

"It soon will be. I don't want that finger bare at this time tomorrow. Question for you. While you are working tomorrow, I want to take Marleigh with me to buy something special. Are you okay with that? My driver is picking me up at noon for my doctor appointment. I can take her with me for the day."

"Really? That would be wonderful. I know she'll love hanging out with her favorite person."

"I love her. I'm going to really be her Dada!" he yelled.

As if Marleigh heard him, the baby monitored chirped and Marleigh starting whimpering on the other end.

"I guess she's up and probably hungry."

Angel moved from his lap and walked naked to the bathroom, grabbing shorts and a t-shirt from her dresser drawer on her way.

"I'll go get her," he offered.

"She'll probably want you anyway. I guess she's like her mother because all I ever want is you too. You get her and we'll share our news with her. I love you," Angel said before walking back into the bathroom.

Getting up, he found clean pants and a t-shirt and raced to Marleigh who was now screaming at the top of her lungs. When she saw him leaning over her crib, she did the most remarkable thing, again. She called his name like only she can.

"Dada, dada, dada."

She raised her arms and he picked her up. When she laid her head on his shoulder and wrapped her little arms around his neck and held on, he couldn't wait to give new meaning to her calling him Dada.

21

The casino and hotel grand opening were well underway. The party that included all of their family and friends was live and entertaining. Some of the biggest celebrities from around the world were present for the party the night before the actual opening. They would all get a first glance at the casino before anyone else so that they could enjoy the place before the public has access. Though no games would be played tonight, everyone would get a tour before they returned the next day to play the slots and gaming tables.

Horace stood on the stage in his all-black attire; black tuxedo with black shirt and gold accessories, with a microphone in his hand. He was patiently waiting for Torrence to make his way through the crowd in his black tuxedo and crisp white shirt.

Looking out over the crowd, everyone in attendance was in their best. The women were glitter and glammed up while the men were dressed to impress.

The world's favorite and most famous DJ was playing music that kept the crowd on the dance floor. Two of the best caterers in the world worked together to prepare the food for the sit-down dinner. With the formal dinner hour officially over, the real fun was about to begin.

There were over a thousand people in attendance and seated in groups of eight around the tables that were decorated in gold and black. Adding to the elegance were the thousands of white roses everywhere, including a wall of roses that also served as the backdrop for photo ops all night.

With everyone looking their best, he still only had eyes for his fiancé. Angel sat at the head table to his left with Marleigh who bounced happily in her lap in her red dress, with white tights and matching red shoes. The red and white ribbons were the cutest. That was his little girl. When it came time to decide what Marleigh would wear tonight, he was ecstatic that Angel asked his opinion. He picked out the red dress. Angel noted it was a perfect choice.

His eyes panned around the room as folks began retaking their seats when he tapped the microphone. There was more to be said before the rest of the evening turned to a serious party.

"Good evening, everyone. Thanks for taking your seats. I have been picked to give tonight's thank you speech, so here it goes. Tonight, is the culmination of a lot of work. Torrence and I started with one casino in Las Vegas. That was the beginning of fulfilling a dream we had back in our college days. Now, we're here, about to open up our third casino in a few years. We are blessed. As Torrence always says, we were favored from birth. I believe that. For a lot of years, I didn't know what my life would be like."

When he began thinking about his childhood, Horace felt himself getting choked up. He cleared his throat. Then he felt a soft hand slide into his. Angel felt his apprehension. He smiled over at her knowing that if anyone outside of Torrence knew him well, it was her. Before he could begin to talk, Marleigh pulled at his jacket wanting to leave Angel's arms to be in his. He never missed a chance to hold her and make her smile. Once she was in his arms and fought him for the microphone, everyone laughed, especially when she leaned forward and tried to talk in it. In two days, she would be a year old. He and Angel were planning a big birthday party for her.

"Are you okay?" Angel leaned over and asked him.

"I am now, baby."

When she started to go back to her seat, he held her hand tight.

"Dada," Marleigh finally said in the mic.

"Yes, baby. It's Dada. Let's see. Where was I? I had a rough childhood. As a teenager, I met Torrence and his family. They took me in and led and guided me toward success. Torrence and his parents are family. Before them, I had a family like all of you did. I'm happy to say that my sisters, Liza and Lisa are here and so is my mother. Wave y'all!" he shouted to them.

"Woohoo!" the crowd cheered.

"Hey, big brother!" Lisa and Liza cheered together.

His mother blew a kiss his way. He was happy that they talked through the issues that kept him away from them for years. Not anymore. He was happy that they were sticking around for a few more days to attend Marleigh's birthday party. He was finally having the family he's always wanted.

"Torrence is my best friend in the entire world. He and his friends welcomed me into their inner circle. I am encouraged and inspired to be a greater, better version of the man I was the day before. I want to give a special thank you to Carter Garrison and his wife, Sienna. If you want to know a man who never gives up, it's Carter. When he said he would never give up on being the man his wife deserved, he meant that. He vowed to never let go of her; and he hasn't. Torrence's wife Reese is here tonight. They embrace me, check up on me and

Reese sets me straight when I'm wilding out. I appreciate and need that. My friend Dexter and his wife Alyssa are here. That there is a man who claims what he wants and goes for it, especially when it comes to his wife and kids. Up next is, Delvin or DJ "Black" Michaels and his wife Avalon. They survived ups and downs that may have caused a less strong couple to go their separate ways. I have learned from him that betting on myself is how I win. He did and all he does is win, win, win! Our very esteemed mayor, Tucker Glass and his wife Nichelle are here and as you can see, expecting a baby. He's taught me to never tangle with him. There is only room for two, well three now, when it comes to love but it's the kind of entanglement he enjoys. I admire him, his career and his life."

"Yes!" someone in the crowd yelled. "Cheers to the best mayor Chicago has ever had!"

"I'm with you on that, now that I live in Chicago, too. Let me address something very important. Here me out now! For all of you trying to be my friend because I will soon be an in-law to him, no freebies to his matches. I'm speaking of Joey *"The Dreads"* Kincaid who is here with his wife, Marlow. They have shown me that a crash isn't always a bad thing if you're crashing into the love of your life. The idea is to survive to love again, and again and then again. At the same table is his brother, and our favorite expert on security as well as a master in the wrestling ring, Carlos Kincaid and his lovely wife Everly. Not even a wild leaked story filled with lies could deter their love which was meant to be. They got back on their path to love and they are great examples for me. Last, but not least at all, is this woman right here with me, Angel. A few weeks ago, she made me the happiest man I could ever be when she said yes to being my forever wife. Nothing prepared me for the rush of emotions that I now know were love at first sight when I met her. Nothing in my life until that moment said that I would ever settle down and make someone else a priority, even over myself. She is why I breathe. She is why I push every day to keep standing. She and this little girl in my arms is why I live and breathe now. I'm not sure I would be here and in love if it were not for her. I never knew what I was chasing in life until I looked up and discovered she and Marleigh here are what I've been seeking and didn't know it. Now that I have them, I've made the greatest gamble of my life. It's a gamble of love. I know casinos. I know gambling, but I didn't know love. Together they make up who I am and now, I am whole. Because of Angel and Marleigh, I am loved like never before. I'm thankful that I can stand with them before you today and say, dreams do come true. I'm speaking about a dream of a perfect career and the dream of a perfect life. This casino has been my baby for a long time. Torrence and I put our all into this casino to make it the best one yet. Each new venture is greater than the last. I can also declare that this is just the beginning for us. The best is still yet to come. Thank all of you for being here to celebrate our success tonight. Most of all, I'm thankful for our very own brat-pack that we've labeled, the *Brothers of Chi-Town*. We truly are family. We truly are brothers. We live and love hard. Because of that, we are living our best lives. Thanks for being here. Please continue to enjoy the food, fun and music tonight. Tomorrow evening, once you put the kiddies to bed, come back and be the first to enjoy the latest *Montiel Avage Hotel and Casino*, Chicago East location. *Welcome!*

22

Asia Wingate stood from her seat in the back of the room, happy that Horace's speech to the crowd was over. She was tired of hearing about how much in love he was. She wanted to toss up her dinner. How dare he declare his love for a woman he's only known months? He's known her for years and knew her every which way possible to man. Yet, she wasn't the one wearing an engagement ring that blinded her from the front of the room. From where she sat and focused on Angel's finger, the large diamond was exquisite.

Asia hated that she wasn't the woman who was the focus of Horace's stupid grin and words of love, love, love. She was over it. She'd come all the way from Las Vegas to reclaim her man, only to find that he wasn't as lost as she thought he was. Another woman had found her. Any hope she had was dashed when she saw how Horace looked at Angel. They were undoubtedly in love. Nothing was going to mess that up.

Her friends, Pamela, Issa, Lynette stood with her. They probably thought that she would be too embarrassed to stay when on their flight from Vegas, all she talked about was getting Horace back. She was all set to work hard at convincing him that now that his new casino was up and running, he needed to return with her to Vegas. They needed to talk about taking their sex-only friendship to the next level. She wanted more with him. Making them an official couple was on her agenda. It was now obvious that her agenda and his did not match. He'd already found his forever woman.

Feeling the angst of the situation, she needed him. At least she did before she arrived in Chicago. Horace was the only man who could help her get her hands on millions of dollars. There were stipulations to getting it that she didn't have time to convince and trust another man with that information. She didn't get far from the table when Pamela tapped her on the arm.

"He's coming this way. If you're trying to get out of here without engaging with Horace, it's too late. He's seen you."

Asia exhaled and turned around to face Horace the minute he walked up to her. On his arm was his beautiful fiancé. She wanted to hate her, but couldn't. From far away she was beautiful. Close up, she was drop-dead gorgeous. Asia was jealous. She worked hard to make sure it didn't show on her face. She was the queen of fake smiles. She plastered one on and held it.

"Asia," Horace said walking up to her with that same cocky grin that had starred in so many of her sexy, amorous dreams, both asleep and wide awake.

"Horace. How are you?" she asked.

"I'm great. I'm glad you and your friends could make it. Ladies, it's good to see you all again."

"It's been a minute. I guess you really aren't coming back to Las Vegas now, huh?" Pamela asked.

Asia poked her friend when her eyes landed on and stayed on Angel.

"This is my fiancé, Angel. Baby, this is Asia Wingate. She's a friend from Las Vegas. These are her friends, Pam, Issa and Lynette."

"It's nice to meet you all," Angel said.

"Likewise," Asia acknowledged. "Horace? Asia? You call me Asia now. What happened to Ace? I'm still her. It's been years since I've heard you call me by my actual name. I guess you've moved on and so we're back to being formal," Asia noted.

The look on Horace's face went from happy to suddenly turn flat and emotionless. She had touched a nerve.

"Now is not the time. How are your brothers and sister?" he asked.

"Um, let's see – Jaxon is still a struggling musician and singer on what I call, the new chicken circuit. He's still trying to find that one break that will have everyone knowing his name. You know he's all about winning hearts."

"He'll make it. I already know it," Horace said.

"If you say so. My sister, Essence, she still dreams of having her exclusive jewelry business. You know, she's all about that diamond, her favorite gem. My brother, Kingston, just quit his job as club manager for the biggest night club in Las Vegas. He still believes that there is something bigger for him if he could just get one foot up. He wants to be the biggest club owner on the west coast. As you can see, they're all good," she replied facetiously.

"And what about you, Ace? What are you up to these days?" Horace asked.

"You know me. I never met a poker table I couldn't win at. I'm not quite a high roller yet, but not many people can go against me at a table."

"Cool," he said.

"Are you all enjoying the festivities?" Angel asked.

Though she was trying to be nice, Asia couldn't do it. The woman has stolen her man with all of her model looks.

209

She looked to her friends and decided she was over being nice. Horace knew what was about to happen. He wouldn't be able to stop her. She was still the hard-ass, loud-mouth he knew. Just because his woman is nice and sweet, that didn't mean that she had to be the same.

"I thought I would be enjoying myself. I came here for a purpose and then discovered that the purpose had already made other plans. So, Horace, does she know about me and you?"

Making a point, Asia pointed her finger first at him and then back at herself.

"Asia, I already said now is not the time."

"What? You got here, fell in love in what a few months? Yet, you left me in Vegas thinking that you were coming back to me. Imagine my surprise to see you in love and all that. Is that your daughter? When did that happen?" Asia asked, pointing to where the woman he pointed out as his mother was holding the baby in red that he'd been holding on the stage.

Horace huffed at her. Back in Vegas, they loved playing the battle of wits with each other. She was ready for him. Before he could speak, Angel stepped in front of him, putting space between them. It was clear she had spunk. Perhaps, Angel wasn't as angelic as her name spoke to.

"Okay, before you try to go in on him, just know that I know who you are. Even after he said now wasn't the time, you're still attempting to make it the time. I won't assume, but you're trying to be disrespectful. I know who you've been to Horace. He's told me about his life in Vegas. You probably thought that I didn't know. He's shared who he was with me; all of it."

"Oh, did he now? Did he tell you about all the women besides me? Did he explain how he treats each one as if they are the one?" Asia asked.

"He told me that he has always been clear about his intentions. Is that why you came here? You came to get Horace back? I'm sorry, he's not available for anything anymore that doesn't involve me. We're being nice and cordial. I can see by your mannerism that you have a different agenda. If you have unfinished business, it's only in the form of words. Anything else is over," Angel declared.

Asia sucked her teeth at the woman who clearly had balls bigger than Horace's.

"What? A cat has your tongue, Horace? Your woman is answering for you?"

"You can address me directly," Angel said, curtly

"Oh?" Asia asked.

He doesn't need to address a woman when it comes to an issue. He's got me for that. I don't go quietly into the night. I talk back. Whatever your plans, you'll have to go back to Vegas and come up with a new one. This one here, is mine. He is not to be confused with someone who used to be yours in whatever way that was that is no more. It was nice to meet you. Enjoy your night and your flight back to Las Vegas," Angel said.

Asia looked to Horace who hunched his shoulders.

"What she said. She's my woman and like she said, she talks back. Have a nice night, life and flight Asia. I'm sorry you wasted your time. Baby, let's dance," he said to Angel.

Asia watched them dance off, leaving her with her mouth hung wide open. When Pamela reached up and pushed her chin up to close her mouth, Asia swatted her hand away.

"What will you do now? Horace was your only chance to get your hands on your share of your grandfather's money. His will was very clear about what you had to do in order to get your share. You have six months. You and your brothers and sisters

211

each have six months. Yours begins first because you drew the shortest straw. You could have had it with Horace because you have history. You could lose ten million dollars if you don't act fast. I know you were planning to fight for him, but let's be real, every part of him loves that woman. He's not going anywhere. We've all seen how he looks at her. Look at him now. He only has eyes for her. That's not going to change," Lynette added.

Asia was thinking the same thing. She should have wished them well instead of trying to antagonize Horace. She was hoping she could enlighten his fiancé about him, but it was clear, she already knew his past with her. It was a ploy to come between them. Her hope had been that he kept who he used to be from Angel. That wasn't the case. He was calm and Angel was patient. It was time she let go of her dreams of them getting back together. She needed a new plan. If she didn't come up with a new one, her house of cards was going to fall down with her underneath of it, crushed for life.

"I'm tired of playing those card games thinking that one day, I am going to play the one poker game that would set me up for life. Ten million dollars is more than any card game could ever pay out."

She took out her cell phone to call for a car service.

"Are we leaving?" Issa asked.

Asia turned and headed for the door of the casino event hall.

"There is no need for us to spend the night in Chicago. I never liked this city anyway. Don't have to worry about me coming back," she said.

Her pace quickened in order to get to the elevator to go to the room that had been reserved for her with her invitation to the gala. Her time here wasn't wasted. She finally understood that she and Horace were over. She didn't need to wait on him.

"We're flying back tonight without flight reservations?" Lynette inquired.

"With this body, I can get us tickets to Peru in a second. Surely, I can get us on a flight out of here tonight and back to Vegas. Sin City is where I belong. I need to get with my siblings to come up with a master plan of how we can work together to get the money our grandfather, that we never knew existed, left us."

"Well, Asia. He didn't leave it for you. He's making you jump through hoops to get it just to spite your mother and your father, whom he hated. Your grandfather, Charles Laslow, was a rich bastard. He died and left your mother, his only daughter, nothing. What he did was set a game in motion to mess with her head. I don't think that he believed any of you would be able to fulfill the terms of his will. He was expecting forty million dollars would be left on the table to go to his pets and a few favorite charities."

They reached the elevator and the door opened. Asia put her room key in and the elevator began to climb to the sixth floor. Her wicked smile was a reflection back to her in the golden, mirrored walls of the elevator.

"I don't really care who he was. What he did to my mother was horrible. The fact that my brothers and sister and I never met him was clearly a blessing. Be that as it may, I want my ten million dollars. Getting back to sin city is where I will find the sucker to play a role to help me get my money. After that, I'll simply drop him like he stole something from me."

"Who is this mysterious man," Issa asked.

"I don't know yet. I do know he's not here in Chicago. Any more time here is a waste. Let's pack and get away from here. These double D's on my chest will get us anywhere we need to be. That place happens to be Las Vegas. If anyone was created to be in that city, it's me. I am sin and sin is me. I just need to be a rich sinner."

"Do you have anyone in mind?" Pamela asked.

"Not at all. I have six months to secretly audition a few men. If nothing else, it will be fun sinning with a few hot guys until I find one so wrapped up in all of this body that he won't realize I'm playing him until I'm done. I play to win. They don't call me Ace of Spades for nothing."

The doors of the elevator may have closed, but Asia saw an opening to becoming rich. She would never have to play another game of poker unless she wanted to. There was a ten-million-dollar pot on the line. She would get it by any means necessary even if she had to kiss a few frogs to get to her temporary prince charming. Unbeknownst to her friends, she had someone in mind. They'd had a one-night-stand a few weeks ago. She was into it until she found out what he did for a living. Could she overlook what he called a job but she called extracurricular activities?

When the door finally opened, she walked ahead of her friends. She hid from them the sinister smile on her face. A plan was forming in her head. She was *Ace* – the most important card and the worthiest in the deck. Her life was the same way. Though adding to that a little bit of wickedness would make her irresistible to any man, it was Dakota Croft who was going to help her make her dreams come true; whether he wanted to or not. She was ready. She could only hope that his fine ass was ready too!

Get ready for a new series based out of Las Vegas, also known as Sin City. First up in the four-book series, *House of Cards*, will be *Ace of Spades*.

Asia "Ace" Wingate is being given the chance of a lifetime to go from barely making it, to living a lavish life in the city that showed her that using what she has to get what she wants became her mantra. When she meets Dakota Croft, a Las Vegas "Gigolo", she gets more than she bargained for. Just when she thinks she's playing him like a masterful card shark, she discovers that she's the one with her cards stacked on the table and Dakota is the man who has a plan to topple it over until it comes falling down.

One steamy night after another is the name of Ace's game to get to what she wants; ten million dollars. Dakota is playing a different game. His is called, win, never lose and only withdraw when she's satisfied because he's playing for keeps.

Come with Ace on a rollercoaster ride in a game of money, power and respect to see if the woman who usually wins can outsmart the one man she underestimated.

Book 1, Ace of Spades, in the *House of Cards* series, is available now for preorder at www.amazon.com/dp/B0DSZGZYDG

Following, *Ace of Spades*, get ready for the stories of her siblings in, *Jack of Hearts, Queen of Diamonds* and *King of Clubs*.

Sin City will never be the same again with the Wingates on a mission to make Las Vegas bow down and salute them as they make it to the top by any sexy means possible!

Never Can Say Goodbye

Book editor, Taryn Novack turned the idea of falling at someone's feet into her personal nightmare. She'd met attorney, Adrian Jarreau a few times in her aunt's New York Apartment building and found the man irresistible. His hard body wasn't the only 'hard' part of him that she was able to lay her eyes on when she tripped and fell at his feet with him dressed only in a towel wrapped around his hips and nothing else. She could have gotten away with her dignity in place until she decided to look up from his feet to...

Adrian knew that Taryn had been avoiding him since that fateful day that he couldn't remove her and his most embarrassing moment. With her being back in New York after the passing of her aunt, they are thrusts together in more ways than one. Moment gone, their whirlwind affair is about to come to an end and she's set to return to Paris. Can she say goodbye and walk away from him without looking back or ever looking up again?

Secure your copy in January 2025 as a download, exclusively on Kindle Unlimited at www.cherylbarton.net.

Island Embers series.
Hunger for You
Desire for You
Thirst for You

What happens on the islands is supposed to stay on the islands but not when it comes to the Blackstone brothers who don't care who knows about their openly and unwavering love for their perfect women.

Preorder book 2 of the, *Island Embers* series, *Desire for You*

https://www.amazon.com/dp/B0DL4MKVRT

About **Desire for You**

Byrum Blackstone is considered the one Blackstone brother who could not be tamed by any woman, no matter how salaciously desirable she is. That is, until he finds himself vulnerable to the one woman he should stay far away from; his executive assistant, Keiko Lee.

In the midst of fighting for her freedom and for custody of her son, Keiko vows to never trust another man with her heart. What she didn't expect was for her boss to offer her wicked, blood pressure spiking, hotter than she's ever known before nights of passion that stir her body and her heart back to life.

Neither Byrum nor Keiko are willing to admit their true feelings as the bigger problem of losing their careers overshadows how bittersweet newfound love could be not just in the present, but in the foreseeable future.

Hunger for You, Book 1 of the _Island Embers_ series

Tellum Blackstone was entranced the moment his eyes landed on Cheyenne Reddick and her magnetic beauty. In her eyes, arms, and heart, he thought he'd found forever. A rift between their fathers had him questioning what kind of real love could be torn apart with a line drawn in the sand.

Cheyenne never thought that she would meet the perfect man until she did in Tellum. He exuded the kind of charm, kindness, and simmering heat that had her mind, body, and soul sizzling like no man had ever done before. To her dismay, a ticking time bomb of epic proportion, in the form of her father, brought about an ultimatum for her to choose a man she loves from a family he detests or lose his love and support forever.

At Secret Whisper, a romantic island resort owned by Tellum, Cheyenne finds that his passion-infused hunger for her easily penetrated her paper-thin resistance. Their desire for each other reignited an insatiable appetite that no woman in her right mind could fight.

Tellum put his all into their red-hot kisses and explosive days and nights of seduction. He needed to find a way to overshadow the risk they were taking in discovering if their love was worth fighting for.

Catch up on book 1, **_Hunger for You_**
www.amazon.com/dp/B0CQZG6CXK

Get all 8 books in the Brothers of Chi-Town series. Here are the first 7

I Can't Let Go, Book 1

Carter Garrison vowed to love, honor and cherish his wife, Sienna, forsaking all others, something he forgot to do during a weekend of fun, bad company and poor judgement. Sienna Garrison never dreamed her college sweetheart, Carter, whom she pledged her life to, would break her heart and when he did, she moved out and moved on - or tried to. What better occasion is there than a friend's wedding to stir up old feelings and memories of love, intense passion and nights of sensual titillation. Gazes from across a room after almost two years apart revealed depths of love that had never died. Seeing Sienna again reminded Carter of what he'd lost and he vowed to never let go by doing whatever he could to get his wife back even if it included begging and pleading. Is Sienna ready to forgive and take a chance on life again with the only man she'd ever really loved? When Carter brings on the charm and turns up the heat, no woman is immune, especially Sienna.

Swagger and Baggage, Book 2

It's not a coincidence that casino owner, Torrence Allen, ran into his college sweetheart, Reese Michaels again; it's fate. As his memories unfold, he had tried everything to keep her in his life and his bed back then and failed at both. She wasn't ready for him then, but he hopes she is ready for him now.

Reese Michaels never thought she'd see Torrence again. Their split in college was dramatic and hurtful and still, no man had been able to win her heart. She considered herself the permanent third wheel to friends who had found love and marriage. Their whirlwind affair, quickly turned into love just as it suddenly crashed and burned when a woman shows up to claim Torrence as hers. When it's also revealed that this woman isn't the only 'other woman', Reese finds herself left with a broken heart, shattered love, and dreams of forever beyond her reach. How did she not know about the other part of Torrence's active and amorous life?

Torrence isn't ready to give up on having Reese in his life after his deceit. He finds himself in the fight of his life to finally have the love and commitment he wanted only with her. His swagger had always won women over, but it's his baggage that's causing his life to spiral out of control and he could once again find himself without the woman he has always loved.

Claiming His Child, Book 3

Business magnate Dexter Patterson refused to let anything keep him from checking off all of the boxes equating to achievement in life to prove that though he came from a rough childhood on the south side of Chicago, he still thrived and became a success. Looking around at those closest to him, Dexter found that he was still missing something...Love.

When aspiring model, Alyssa Kincaid met Dexter, she couldn't get enough of his sexual magnetism, fiery nights of passion, and secret rendezvous. She thought they were headed toward forever when a surprising call from him ended what they had causing her to leave Chicago, taking with her a secret.

Dexter thought that no woman could ever tame him, not even Alyssa who entranced him with her sexy body, smoky, sultry voice and untamed desire. Too little, too late, he realized he'd made a mistake by walking away and then she was gone. Time and distance didn't diminish the chemistry between them and the child Alyssa carried and never told him about had him in the fight of his life to win back her heart and the chance to have the family he'd always wanted.

Will Alyssa continue to curse kismet when Dexter suddenly reappears in her life or will she believe that his yearning for her isn't just because of their child, but because when she left Chicago, she took his heart with her?

Always Bet on Black, Book 4

Sexy, debonair, Delvin "DJ" "Black" Michaels, left Chicago as a man in search of a better life than the one he had where everyone knew him as "Black". He met a woman, fell in love, and then she turned out to be someone he didn't really know when her scandalous life ruined his career.

Avalon Hart had lived her life on the edge, making do the best way she knew how even if it meant scheming men out of their hard-earned money. She learned how to survive from the streets and she was a woman who had a way with men that got her whatever she wanted, that was until she encountered DJ Michaels in Chicago, a man from her past whom she had once easily swayed to her desires. She realized early that the man she encountered in New York had grown immune to her tricks, even the ones she learned how to do in bed that he loved so much.

DJ and Avalon are on a roller coaster ride to love and neither knew it. He had a lot to lose if he let Avalon get too close to him again. This time, whatever she was plotting, he was ready to take her down, even if it meant losing his heart in the process.

He was betting on "Black" for the win, but so was Avalon, in her own way. There was no telling who would end up on top, but one thing was for sure – the road to getting there was going to be filled with hot, sexy fun, a pair of handcuffs and a whole lot of sensuality that neither could resist!

It Takes Two to Tangle, Book 5

Councilman Tucker Glass, a native of Chicago, has set his eyes on the biggest prize, that of Mayor of the city he has loved all of his life. At thirty-nine, his career spans back many years as a City Council member and then most recently, as City Council President. His resume reads like a ratings-topper novel full of accomplishments that make him more than qualified for the job, but what he wants to avoid is the drama that could block his path to the mayor's mansion. He's always been a strait-laced politician, but his personal life could spawn a real-life reality show complete with hair pulling, tongue-lashing and accusatory finger pointing which would all occur in the first episode. Tucker wasn't expecting his past to come back to haunt him just as he'd found the woman who was making his life complete. He would do anything to keep her in his life, but is he willing to give up his run for the mayor's office to keep that love in-tact? Nichelle Michaels didn't know that love could be so right until she met and fell in love with Tucker Glass, a man fourteen years older and wiser than her, but who showed her how a man should treat a woman, and that's after she spent the past year testing the water between how a man loves and how a woman loves. Now that she knows what she wants, a woman from Tucker's past could ruin her perfect love. Tucker and Nichelle are in love, but is he willing to risk his chance at being Mayor because his ex-wife, or the woman he thought was his ex-wife, wants to now be First Lady of Chicago? Was he really ready to tangle with a woman who specialized in drama every day on television as the star on the nation's number one reality show? Tucker may be ready for Chicago, but is Chicago ready for the drama that comes along with the popular politician?

Crashing Into Love, Book 6

His name is Joseph Kincaid and while most call him Joey, the women of Chicago call him a variety of sexy epithets that are too salacious to utter in public. He's a professional wrestler who is unmatched in the ring, untamed in his response to confrontation and unleashed when it comes to his bedroom proclivities, bringing women pleasure beyond their amorous fantasies. For the second time in her life, Marlow Warren was responsible for an accident that altered someone's life. The first time, she ran to avoid bringing disgrace to her family while hiding from her past, but this time, she's all about making amends to the man whose life she ruined. Everything changed when Joey and Marlow's lives collided. It wasn't all bad. Hurt, anger and unending apologies turned into lust, desire and unbridled cravings, something neither of them could fight. When Marlow's past arrives in a threatening way, Joey knew he would risk his life to protect her because he was now fighting for more than a future back in the ring; he was ready to fight for love.

Carlos Kincaid is an irresistible, rugged loner who is the epitome of that good guy who finishes last when it comes to women. His life is finally on track when Everly Robinson, his Achilles' heel returns to Chicago to turn his world upside down. She stirs up memories of their inexhaustible, hot, steamy, lust-filled nights that he thought were long gone.

Everly chose the wrong man one time too many in her life. She finds herself on the run from two dangerous men, one who conned her into leaving the only love she's ever known and the other whom she calls her father. In desperate need of help, she escaped a mental and physical prison to go in search of the one man she trusts and has always loved.

Carlos is frustrated that old feelings could lead him back into the arms of the woman he needed to hate in order to move on. He couldn't tell if her story was filled with lies or truths. Against his better judgement, he's ready to risk his heart and his life for a woman who once betrayed him and his love.

Brothers of Chi-Town Series
I Can't Let Go
Swagger and Baggage
Claiming His Child
Always Bet on Black
It Takes Two to Tangle
Crashing into Love
Leaks, Lies, Lust and Love
Love's Gamble

Get the entire 5-book series, The Sullivans of Montana, now available for your reading pleasure at
https://www.amazon.com/dp/B09M41D76N?binding=kindle_edition&ref=dbs_dp_rwt_sb_pc_tkin

The Sullivans of Montana
Home for Thanksgiving
The Way You Love Me
On the Right Track
Three's a Crowd
The Law of Love

Stand Alone Romance
Snowbound
Cupid's Arrow
One Wish
His Halloween Promise
Holly for Christmas
A Better Man
Bossy
Un-Break My Heart
Love on Top
Take a Knee
Love at First Sight
My First Love
Black Love
A Younger Man
One Moment in Time
The Lake House
True Lies or True Love
When I Think of You
And Then There Was You
Baby, Come Back
Unforgettable
The Power of Seduction
Seize the Moment
A Christmas Wish
It Should Have Been You
The Christmas Layover
The Sweetest Revenge
The Sweetest Temptation
The Diner
Dashing Through the Snow
A Trick and a Treat
Love Therapy
*Mister Christmas

Upcoming Romance Releases

Sons of a Sullivan

*Wrath of a Sullivan

Upcoming Urban Drama

*Amerikka

Christian Romance Series

When God Says Yes
Rescue Me
Release Me
*Restore Me

Inspirational Series

Encouraging Words From One Sister to Another
One Sister Away, Volume 1
One Sister Away, Volume 2
One Sister Away, Volume 3
One Sister Away, Volume 4

Inspirational Standalone
A Letter to My Mother
Straightening Her Crown

About the Author

Cheryl Barton lives in Maryland and in her spare time she loves to read espionage, crime and romance novels, cook, watch Sci-fi movies, spend time with family and friends and enjoy Maryland steamed crabs.

Cheryl is the author of over forty romance novels, four inspirational novels and is proud of six book compilation projects with several other incredible women.

Cheryl was a 2019 Finalist for the Emma Award given by Romance Slam Jam and a 2018 Finalist for the Literary Trailblazer of the Year award by the Indie Author Legacy Award.

Cheryl's books are available on her website as well as www.bn.com, www.amazon.com and www.kobo.com

Connect with Cheryl Barton
Author Cheryl Barton website
www.cherylbarton.net
Amazon Author Page
www.amazon.com/author/cherylbarton
Instagram: @cherylbartonauthor
Facebook: @authorcherylbarton
Threads: @cherylbartonbooks@threads.net

www.ingramcontent.com/pod-product-compliance
Lightning Source LLC
Chambersburg PA
CBHW030329030726
47499CB00003B/697